C000003558

FCON '15

GodBomb! First Published in 2015

Published by The Sinister Horror Company

Cover design by Vince Hunt.

ISBN
978-0993279393

What They Said

"GodBomb! paints a huge panorama on a tiny canvas. Set entirely in one location, a community hall in a rural town, Kit Power uses the social microcosm of a Born Again Christian Revivalist meeting to explore a whole macrocosm of social and theological issues. As the stories of the believers and non-believers, held captive by a zealous suicide bomber, play out, the author examines how the need for absolute certainty in a secular society often erodes the personal redemption offered by blind faith. This is a violent and angry book but you will not put it down without being touched by the characters and their struggles as it hurtles towards a truly explosive finale."

Jasper Bark, award winning author of Prime Cuts,
Stuck On You and Bloodfellas

"Tense, thrilling and challenging. An explosive debut that shatters expectations."

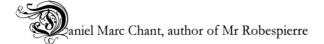

Daniel Marc Chant, author of Mr Robespierre

"This cat's name says it all--"Power". His writing is like lighting a fuse, not the hissy super loud kind you see in cartoons...this is a slow burning quiet fuse. long enough that you almost forget about it until the explosion removes your face and limbs. He writes smart and honest and with no apologies."

ohn Boden, author of DOMINOES

"The result is dark and explosive. I can but congratulate Mr Power on this little masterpiece, an emotional rollercoaster that left me quite incapable of even drinking my tea – I just couldn't tear my eyes away from the text."

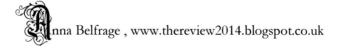nna Belfrage , www.thereview2014.blogspot.co.uk

Dedication

For my father, who is quite simply the smartest man I know. Thank you for teaching me early the power of the question. I have never forgotten it, and guess what? It still works.

And for his mother, my Grandma Annie – 103 years old. I love you, Grandma. I find your lack of faith inspiring.

Contents

The Players

The Players

THE PREACHER – Male/43/Preacher

DEBORAH – Female/20/Angry

CHRIS – Male/19/Seeker

TWITCH – Male/30's/Alcoholic

KATIE - Female/16/Churchgoer

ALEX – Female/18/Just finished A-levels

EMMA – Female/27/Eight and a half months pregnant

MIKE – Male/37/Sax player

"You shall not put the LORD your God to the test..." - Deuteronomy 6:16

"If God does exist, he's a sadist." - Annie Baume

Author's Note:

The following story is set in North Devon, England and takes place on July 23rd, 1995.

1995. Blur Vs. Oasis is coming to a head. Thatcher is history, the Tories adrift in the long, drawn out dog days of the Major years. The month before, The Stone Roses pulled out of their headliner slot at the Glastonbury festival, and a well-respected but relatively lesser known band called Pulp got their moment to shine. They took it. Here in North Devon, we live in a land so close to Springsteen's vision of heaven – "Cold beer at a reasonable price, and no fuckin' cell phones!"

By March of the following year, the Dunblane school shooting will effectively end access to handguns for the entire UK population, but right now, it's still possible to own and shoot a pistol, if you're prepared to jump through enough hoops.

And somewhere in there, I attend my first and last born again church revival meeting.

What follows is as close as I can get to a faithful rendition of what occurred. Details will be wrong. Names too, almost certainly. Nevertheless, this is as near as I can get to a true history of that day.

Almost none of it happened. But this is how I remember it.

Leviticus

have questions."

There's a murmur, a ripple that rolls through the congregation.

"I wanna know..."

He drifts off, uncertain. Hesitant. But **the preacher** can see the kid's eyes, and they are bright, alert. Intense. *This could be the big one*, thinks the preacher, *right here. Barely five minutes into the service, this kid could open the floodgates.*

Play it slow.

"You are amongst friends, son. Try not to be shy." Smiling, open.

The kid nods, swallows, tries a smile of his own.

"What do you want to ask me?"

"I want.. I want to know if you believe God is real. I mean, really real. You know?"

There're a few chuckles at that – some disguised as coughs, but most not. The kid's eyes flick nervously, trying to locate the source of the sound. The preacher doesn't take his eyes off the kid's face, but he tries frantically to send 'shut the heck up' thoughts to the crowd. *Can't they see how scared he is? Don't they understand the importance of what he's really trying to ask?*

"I do understand, son. I do. And yes, I believe God is really real." Smiling, but not laughing. Reassuring. "God is as real as it's possible to be. I know it. May I ask what you think?"

Risky. Always risky, asking a question you don't know the answer to, but he's running on a strong intuition here, indistinguishable from divine guidance. This kid wants to share.

He wants to believe.

There's a long pause. The preacher can see the kid's face working it over, too much feeling and too few words. God bless country education. This boy needs the Lord so badly.

"I don't know, man. That's the honest truth. I thought I did, but now I don't."

The kid's voice is deep, resonant, and as he swallows, the preacher notes a fine layer of stubble on his chin. His eyes have been distant, wandering, but now they turn back to the preacher's, and they are bright and sharp. Focussed. The preacher allows himself a moment to take caution: articulate or otherwise, the kid is smart.

"I came here to find out."

The preacher's smile splits to a grin. He allows his eyes to sparkle, just a little, his voice to waver just so — easy enough, because he's now high as a kite. *Thank you, Lord. Thank you for sending me this lamb, and thank you for giving me the power to help him. All glory to You. All glory to You.*

"Come up here, son. Come up on this stage."

The kid tries to take a step back, but of course he can't, the bench is at his calves. He wobbles a little. The preacher wonders why the kid doesn't take his hands out of his jacket pockets to steady himself instead of digging them in deeper, leaning forward to beat the tipping point. A blush rises on the kid's face. The preacher holds his pose; arm outstretched in welcome, face open and honest.

"God will give you the answers you seek. If you come..."

"You promise?"

The kid is bolt upright now, almost rigid, face rippling with emotions. "I can talk to God? He'll come and talk to me?"

The preacher allows the ghost of a laugh to enter his voice. "He's already here, son. But yes, you'll hear his voice..."

The kid's already moving, stepping out into the aisle. Striding towards the stage, full of energy and purpose.

"I hope you're right, preacher, I surely do."

As he talks, his hands pop from his pocket. The left is just a closed fist, but the right contains a lump of black plastic, with a wire running up his sleeve.

The preacher feels his smile freezing on his lips, his face become numb, his body locking into immobility.

The kid's left hand reaches for his zipper.

"I want to talk to him, preacher. I *need* to talk to him."

The jacket falls open. Underneath, the preacher sees a lunatic tangle of wires and metal and strange grey blocks. The preacher hears some gasps from the front aisle seats as the turned heads take in the view, but it's all happening from a long way away, and still he stands frozen in a statue of welcome. Still the kid advances with terrible pace towards the stage.

"He and I need to have a very serious conversation."

The kid climbs onto the stage slowly, pushing up with his arms before swinging his legs under him. He squats, then stands, and stares the preacher in the eyes. He's shorter, has to look up to make eye contact, but the preacher sees no fear, no nerves.

In fact, he sees very little at all.

"I've got enough explosives strapped to my body here to level this building and kill everyone inside. The first person who tries to run will end you all."

There's a series of gasps, some sobs, nothing louder. *The garden of a thousand sighs*, thinks the preacher, randomly. Then on the heels of that *thank God we said no children. Thank God for that, at least.*

Yes, thank God, no kids, but still, near to a full house. Seventy souls? Eighty?

Dear Lord, what have we stumbled into?

"I've tried, you know."

The kid has turned back to him, conversational, but the little SOB has obviously had some performance training because he's speaking from the diaphragm. The preacher has no doubt that every word is carrying right to the back of the hall.

"I've tried and tried. I've prayed till I cried, preacher, and I've cried till I puked, and you know what?"

He holds up his empty hand and clicks his fingers. In the silence of the hall, the sound echoes like a pistol shot.

"Nothing. Not. A. Thing."

Still conversational, but the preacher can feel a reservoir, an ocean of rage just beneath the surface of that calm.

Dear Lord, help me now. Merciful God, help us all. I pray.

"Well, I finally decided, enough is enough, you know. So, here we are. Here we all are."

He turns to his audience and raises his arms, showing off the device strapped to his chest, letting them all take it in. There's a gasp/sigh/yelp/sob that threatens to erupt into a full-fledged panic, but he lifts his encumbered right hand to his mouth, index finger over his lips, and like a room full of schoolchildren, they fall silent again. Every eye on the lump of plastic.

On the red button held down by his thumb.

This is power, thinks the preacher, and shudders.

"Here's the deal, people. I've had enough of not knowing. Today, we're all going to find out together if this man is telling the truth; if Jesus is the risen Lord, who died for all our sins. One way or another, you will all be witnesses."

He pauses, looking out over the crowd. To the preacher, the boy's gaze seems like gunfire, heads dropping wherever his eyes fall.

"So, this is the experiment. You, God's chosen and true believers, start praying. Tell Him that I want to talk to Him, and tell Him what he should already know: that if He doesn't speak to me, I'm going to kill all of us."

He turns to the preacher.

"Would you like to lead them in prayer?"

But for the first time in his adult life, the preacher can find no words. He merely stands there, frozen, heart hammering sickly in his chest, fear and misery shutting down all thought.

The reply does not come from the preacher, but from the front row.

"No."

Esther

She almost doesn't realise that the word has come from her mouth. She jumps, first at the sound of her own voice, and then again as she looks up at the stage. The bomber has turned his focus on her. The preacher stands behind him; arms still open, face white.

The bomber looks amused. Also furious. She straightens up in her chair, trying to seem defiant, but inside, her gut is churning, mind panicked; whatever wild energy that led her to speak has now deserted her utterly. She's the kid in the class with her hand in the air but no answer, except this time, instead of laughter, there's likely to be a fireball.

"A dissenter?" He manages a laugh, but it's an effort, she thinks, and the result is not good. Unless he was going for creepy, which she doesn't rule out.

He walks over to her and takes a seat on the edge of the stage, keeping the trigger arm straight as he does so. Up close, his face is even worse. His eyes are bright, but dead. The smile looks stitched on, painful. She feels a cramp of fear in her midsection; is aware her heart rate has increased, that she's probably blushing.

Somehow she manages to hold his gaze.

"I like dissent. Encourage it. What's your name?"

"Deborah."

"Well, Deborah, I'd like to know more about you." He nods slowly as he speaks, like she's already agreed with him. "You're clearly very brave, to speak up in such a dangerous situation." He raises the fist with the trigger and leans forward slightly.

She turns her head up, to follow his hand, and he brings the fist down, scarily fast, cracking his knuckles across the top of her head. There's an instant starburst of pain, followed by an ache that spreads across her scalp. She cries out. Gasps close to shouts erupt around her.

"I'm very good at spotting a lie, so tell the truth or I'll hit you again. Do you understand?"

"Yes."

"Do you believe me?"

"Yes."

Crack. This time the blow lands on her forehead, knuckles scraping down to the bridge of her nose. Tears squirt into her eyes. More gasps.

"Do you?"

"Yes!"

His smile widens, becoming genuine. She sees his shoulders relax. She stares at the thumbnail holding down the button in the fist that just hit her. It appears to be winking at her.

"Good! How old are you, Deborah?"

"Twenty."

"And how long have you been a cripple?"

The word burns her, adding more tears to the pain.

"Seven years."

"Speak up, please."

"Seven years."

"I see. What happened when you were thirteen?"

In her fear and pain, the story tumbles out of her, almost a babble of words.

"I was running. I loved to run. I was running to the shop, fast as I could. Used my ears to look for traffic. The car was quiet, so I didn't hear it. Ran right in front of it."

She's told the story many times, but the situation she's in now brings the whole thing back, vividly. The crunch sound, the feeling of being flipped, flying, total disorientation, followed by a thud that seemed to end the world.

Then waking up in a hospital bed. All that pain in her head and back. None in her legs. The sad doctors and the x-rays. The tiny chances of recovery, and the dumb hope that gave her parents. Their fervour sure to secure the miracle. The worm of doubt that grew and grew in her mind as weeks became months became years of legs as meat, as weight, as dead wood.

Her mind is so absorbed with the near total recall that she doesn't even register that he's spoken again, much less hear the words.

The next blow comes in sideways, across her cheek, snapping her head to the side, and her left eye fills with water, temporarily blinded.

"If you keep making me hit you, I might slip." He wiggles his fist at her, the trigger switch flicking back and forth. She hears moans from around and behind. The kid beside her starts grunting in terror, 'mu-mu-mu-mu-mu-mu'. She can see him twitching in his chair in her peripheral vision, his orange shirt seeming to writhe. She forces herself to ignore it, and the frantic shushing sounds his mother/nurse/carer is making.

"I said, why are you here?"

She feels the answer rise, but it's shameful. She hesitates, trying to think of something else to say, some good lie, but he reverses his fist, pulls back, and she has no desire to turn the other cheek.

"My parents. They brought me here. They made me come." *Left me here,* she thinks but does not say. What would be the point? She's obviously alone.

"Why?"

"They think... They're hoping for a miracle. They heard this man sometimes does healings, and they wanted it for me, so they asked... they made me come."

Her insides feel as though they are twisting up at the

memory of this. The implacability of her parents, indifferent to her humiliation at the hand of crank after crank. Their insistence that this could be the one. If only she believed hard enough, if only she...

And underneath, the fear that she *is* somehow to blame. That if her heart were only purer, her faith true...

The bomber swings his stiff arm further back. His index finger uncurls from the black plastic and points at the priest.

"Him?"

"Yes."

"What do you say, preacher? Think you can work a miracle, save this woman, get her up and walking? Perhaps we could all go home early. Do you think?" His eyes never leave hers as he speaks, and Deborah can feel the cruel amusement oozing from him. Under all the fear and all the pain and all the shame and all the confusion, Deborah finds a tiny seed of hatred.

How fucking dare he?

"I'd love to, but..."

"Ah! Do you hear, Deborah? There's a but!" He's trying to smile through his sneer. It's ugly.

"No, really, this is not, ah, conducive to... I mean, look, the healings, they come when God commands me, I don't control it, it's not my power, it's his..."

"Okay, how about the spastic?"

"It's Cerebral Palsy, you ignorant fuck!" The anger shocks her, the words tearing at her throat as they pass through, leaving pain and a faint taste of blood. Her heart is hammering in earnest now, and her veins feel on fire with useless adrenaline.

Where did that come from?

He turns back to her. His face is still, his eyes dead. "Shout at me again like that, Deborah, and I will beat your pretty face until you lose consciousness, or I lose my grip. Clear?"

She nods, the ice-cold bucket of fear mixing with the

heat of her anger. She feels like she might retch.

"Clear?"

"Yes." It's an effort to talk now. Her jaw is swelling along with her lip.

The room falls silent. Deborah can feel the weight of them behind her, the fears of the whole congregation weighing on her shoulders, willing her to not kill them all, to do what this madman wants. She feels her bottom lip trembling as she tries not to burst into tears. She can taste blood in her mouth.

She holds his gaze as he stares, his image clear in one eye, fractal in the other, like a multi-headed monster. Wishing she had the power to jump up from her chair and rip that head off, kick it down the aisle like a football. The thought surprises her with its strength.

"What do you think, Deborah? Do you think he has the power to heal you?"

"No."

"Why not?"

And there's no time to consider, so she simply says, "Because I don't believe in God anymore."

The bomber nods, face grave now. "Why not?"

"Too many of these. Too many like him. I'm still... here."

He nods again, face turning thoughtful, even sad. "Well, I hope for everyone's sake that you're wrong. But at least, come the end, we'll know."

"No." She's weary now, exhausted, the useless adrenaline sludging up her system, but he's made her talk now, and she apparently can't stop.

"Yes. Either God comes, or we all die. And if we all die, we know he's not real. We die knowing the answer that has plagued humanity since..."

"Why not just kill us now? He's not coming." There are some shouts at this, and the preacher draws breath to speak, but the bomber points at him violently with the detonator hand, making him fall silent. His eyes never leave Deborah's face. The grin is back, and it's hateful.

"Let's see, shall we?" He turns to the crowd. "Silent prayer is best. I'm told. Begin. Beseech, reach out with your hearts and minds. Tell God I'm here, and I want to talk to him. The clock is ticking."

He takes them all in, finally turning to face the preacher, who lowers his head quickly, afraid to make eye contact. Deborah feels a wave of disgust, before a revelation slams into her, making her breath catch in her throat.

She lied. She lied to the bomber, and he swallowed it whole. Because Deborah's revelation is this – she does believe in God. She always has done, and that belief has not been changed one bit by any of the charlatans claiming to work in His name. Everything that's happening is God's design.

God is real, and Deborah hates Him.

Her eyes flick back to the bomber, posing with his arms outstretched, eyeballing the crowd, totally unaware of her. *He didn't spot it. He's not as good as he thinks he is.* It feels true, to Deborah, and exciting, but also dangerous.

"Excellent. Let us pray."

Then he walks back over, sits in front of Deborah and leans forward. Deborah shrinks back into the chair, afraid he is going to kiss her, but he places his lips by her ear, and whispers,

"Thank you."

He turns and climbs back to his feet without looking at her again. Deborah, jaw clenched, trembles and sweats. And thinks.

Psalms (I)

The seconds crawl by, but the minutes *fly*. The congregation prays, or they try to. Some of the believers struggle with this hitherto most basic function, whilst some of the sceptics find themselves taking to it like a drunk to whisky, now they finally see the size and shape and depth of their own foxhole.

Many think of escape too, but it's an unprofitable line of enquiry. They are in a single room; no pillars, clear sightlines from the stage to every corner, and the young man does not seem to so much as blink.

At the rear of the hall, the escape thing is a different calculation, because, look: if you're seated in the back row, beloved of loafers and troublemakers from primary school on down, the exit is what, ten feet away? Best not to turn around, best to try and figure it from memory, but yes, ten feet feels right, surely no more than fifteen, and he says he's got enough bang to take out the whole building, of course he does, but how could he possibly know? Enough to take out the front row? Sure. Maybe all the way to the centre aisles, even, but really? The whole building? Especially if you have your back to the blast, moving in the direction of travel, if you can dig it? Okay, maybe you get through the door a little quicker than you thought. Maybe your feet don't touch the ground for the last few inches... but maybe you make it out alive and with a story to tell. Especially if you can get a jump somehow, if that maniac on stage is distracted, even for a few seconds.

Chris, in his rear aisle seat, is certainly alive to these possibilities – it's pretty much all he's thought about since the bomber showed his hand. He can't help risking glances to his left and right, trying to figure out who else this might have occurred to.

It wouldn't be good to be beaten to the punch.

His opposite number seems safe – the male half of a middle-aged couple that has all the true believer hallmarks. The husband looks shocked and scared, but that raw panic that strips a man of everything but the will to survive is not yet manifest. He does not strike Chris as the kind of man that could conceal such a shift if it did come. The civilising presence of his wife may mean it never does.

In front of him, the teenage girl/woman in a leather jacket seems a more likely candidate, but she's either lost in prayer or despair at the moment. Further forward, the odds of misguided survival instinct trumping common sense diminish and absent blind panic, Chris is less worried. Directly in front of him is an old man – seventies, eighties. By the sound of his breathing, there's every chance that he might beat them all to the answer.

Chris is pretty sure no one who doesn't have an aisle seat is in with a prayer, but of course eternal optimism is a curse of the species, so he tries to scope out the other back row denizens for flight risks. So far, so good. The only one that is giving him any concern is the guy right next to him.

The dude is perspiring profusely, and he smells nasty. Fever or something else? One to watch anyway, and Chris does. He watches as close as he can, wondering what might be going on inside that sweaty brow. Hoping that he doesn't blow a gasket.

He's right to worry, because **Twitch** is having a pretty terrible day. His rational mind, warped by many years of substance abuse and justification of same, is now experiencing an external pressure caused by the will of another. Twitch can almost feel himself creaking under the strain. He sort of prays, and it sounds like this:

Please God please I'm sorry God I need a drink God why the fuck did I come here God please get me out God please get me a drink God I swear if you get me out of here I'll check into rehab God please you know I'm telling the truth I'm cured Lord just set me free God oh God I need a drink God what the fuck am I doing here? God...

You get the idea. Round and round and round, each circuit just a little more frantic. And there are physiological consequences of his failure to feed his addiction; a raised heart rate, an inability to fully catch breath. A sweat that begins to coat his dirty skin, making him slick, slippery under his clothes.

Twitch is starting to twitch.

Alex, now, Alex is thinking. Furiously. She went through shock and denial pretty quickly; was done with them before the nutter had finished speaking, and she seems to have skipped pain and guilt entirely. She is absolutely fucked if she's going out like this. No, Alex has moved into casa anger, and she's just fine there, thanks so much.

Still, she takes a moment to contemplate the girl she'd been just a few minutes ago. Pissed off, but a happy kind of pissed off. Sure, she'd been dumped by her girlfriend. Outed by said dumper to her prude parents. Kicked out of home by said parents, and just sat her final A-level exam (which she's pretty sure she aced, despite all the bullshit). But she'd seen the posters for this event, and something inside had just... snapped. Fucking fundy clappies with their bad haircuts and shitty, ripped-off-from-the-US sermons, so blatant they sometimes even slip into the accent (she remembers her drunken rants at The God Channel in the early hours, and wonders briefly how much that had to do with getting dumped) bringing their ugly, dumb, homophobic bullshit to *her* town?

She remembers preparing the glitter bomb – pink paint, extra red glitter, and a little wood glue for consistency. Sewing the extra pocket into her jacket, just big enough for the glass jar. Getting here early. Getting a good aisle seat near the front. Listening to the band warm up without really listening. Wondering if the preacher would go after the gays on his own, or if she'd have to prompt him, and contemplating with a savage joy the look on his face when she flung the sparkling concoction at him and perfectly fucked up his day.

Irony.

She makes a promise to herself-that-was. She swears she'll make it back to her.

Her eyes go back to the stage. Take in the bomber. Her mind runs the situation over. The guy is clearly a maniac. They tend to have a far grander sense of their own abilities than the reality demonstrates. Maybe he's wired his bang up wrong. Maybe he's rigged the trigger wrong, and maybe even if it's rigged right, he doesn't have as much bang as he thinks, and maybe... Well, OK, that's as far as she's gotten, but she's working on it. Thanks to her desire to be as close to the stage as possible, and her need for an aisle seat, she knows she doesn't really have a shot at getting out, unless there's a distraction of fairly major proportions. Besides, that's not what she has in mind.

What she has in mind is that chicken switch. Because the thing is, it doesn't matter who's holding that button down – as long as it is down, the bang can't go off. Alex is not the praying type, but she does fervently hope that she's not the only person in the room to have figured this out. Mr. Mad Bomber is relying on idiot fear to blind people to that very simple truth.

He's not the threat. The trigger is. And he's not even

an especially long streak of piss. It would take, what; two or three people to overpower him completely? Three max. You'd have to be quick, obviously, and close, and someone's job has to be securing the button, but it's absolutely doable. Given the options, Alex thinks it's a pretty fucking good plan.

So Alex is looking for candidates to help her in this endeavour, assuming she can somehow get close to or, even better, *on* that stage. Assuming he stays there and doesn't go walkabout. Assuming some other thing doesn't fuck up and kill them all, but Alex is not about to be swamped by that bullshit, *fuck that noise, kids, let's give ourselves a chance, shall we?* And geographically speaking, her only real candidates are either the preacher or the band.

She eyes up the priest, but what she sees does not inspire confidence. He doesn't look like a man of action, for one. For another, he seems completely thrown. His eyes are tight shut, and his lips are moving, so he's clearly taking the instruction to pray very seriously, and this is, in Alex's mind, a Bad Sign. It's bad because it means that he's not thinking through the threat; that he's bought into the story the arsehole is selling. That's a pity, because out of the entire room, he's the one best placed to make a move.

Alex briefly considers praying for the priest to grow a pair, before deciding it's probably better to focus on tools she knows work – this is no time to start investing capital in unproven hypotheses.

She assesses the band instead. Drums, bass, two guitars, and the sax player. Strictly an instrumental affair. Her heart sinks further as she looks at them. The drummer is staring into space, looking like he's either just pissed himself or is just about to. The three guitarists are actually holding hands; eyes closed, with the bass player crying, great big tears rolling down his cheeks and dripping from his chin onto his instrument.

Standing apart from the group, the sax player also has his eyes closed, but she notices that he's not crying and that his breathing is slow and steady – he could almost be sleeping. Straight back. Hands resting on his sax. He looks... serene. A preposterous word, given the circumstances, but there it is. After the apparently useless priest, he's the closest to the nutter. So it's him she focuses on, all her useless will bent to one thought: *Open your fucking eyes, man.*

Mike prays. Mike has an edge over most here, including even the preacher. Mike doesn't believe. He *knows.* He was a drunk and a drug addict and a bad person, well on his way to an early grave. Mike knows he was bound for destruction. He knows. And it was Jesus who prevented it.

The moment is seared in his mind irrevocably – and how could it not be? It was, after all, the moment of his true birth – the moment he was saved and embraced his purpose as a child of God. The pivot upon which his whole life turns. On some fundamental level, this moment is always with him, endlessly replaying, a source of strength and peace. The sunlight through the dark clouds, the drizzle suddenly warm on his skin, making the hairs on his arm stand up, as the car drove away and the voice spoke in his mind, clear and strong, ringing his whole body like a bell.

Mike, I'm calling you to the kingdom.

He remembers, with a smile ghosting unnoticed across his lips, his reply – 'Sure, God, sure, just, like, give me a little while to get myself sorted, you know...' – and the reply, calm, gentle, firm.

Mike. I'm not calling you tomorrow. I'm calling you now.

And that was that. He found the nearest church service (a born-again ceremony, how could it not be?) declared the Lord and never looked back.

Since then, he has felt God's presence constantly in his life, in every moment he has been aware of God's love, and it has guided his every action and his every thought. This silly boy with his silly bomb can't threaten that. He can't even scratch it. Mike's eyes are closed, hands resting on the cool metal of his sax, and his mind and heart and soul fly free, fly into God's loving arms. He feels no fear and no regrets. *If this is your will, Lord, let it be done.* He thinks, *this could be it. I could really be going.*

He tries not to smile.

Lord, as you will it. I am your instrument, however crude. Your vessel, however unworthy.

I will Mike, I will. I hold you all in my hands. Evil will never win. Nothing can stand against my Love. I hold you all.

Mike does smile at this. He can't help it.

Open your eyes, Mike. Open them, and see clearly.

He does so immediately, and his gaze is pinned by that of a young lady with an aisle seat, three rows back. She's almost handsome, he thinks, and glowing with life the way the young (especially young women) do. Her eyes are blazing. He sees the will of the Lord working in that gaze, and turns his own over to it. His smile broadens momentarily, and he inclines his head, just a fraction.

She does the same, flashing a grin back.

Next to Mike, oblivious to this communication but very aware of the passing of time, the preacher is lost in prayer. At least, he's trying to be. He's subvocalizing the Lord's Prayer over and over, but that's really just a mantra, something for his lips and upper mind to be doing, and yes, something for his audience. Not the congregation, so much — them too — but his real audience, the one that really matters, the kid with the bomb.

It's a kind of meditation (he would never call it such, but it is) and what it does is free his deeper thoughts to wander. And they do. He reaches out into scripture, looking for injunctions against murder, against suicide, most of all, against testing God's will. That seems to be the key. This kid is clearly deranged, perhaps even possessed, but there's at least a surface logic at work. If the kid is telling the truth, there is a chance. If he can inject doubt into the kid's mind about this insane test... if he can somehow convince him that this path he's on will prove nothing, then maybe...

So his thoughts run over scripture (mainly the New Testament – best stay clear of fire, brimstone and vengeance for the moment), but they also head in another direction. He cries out to God with his mind, with an urgency he rarely has before. *Help me, Lord. Help us. Save us. Yours is the power and the Glory. Show your Power. Tell me what to do. Tell me how to stop this.*

Eventually, he feels brave enough to open his eyes. The clock hanging over the door shows 10:27 – almost an hour has passed. *God, give me strength.*

The preacher clears his throat to talk. The boy turns to him.

"May I speak with you?"

Job

Twitch hears this, but it comes to him as if from a great distance. The inside of Twitch is a ball of sweaty heat now, itchy, flaky, dark. Beneath his closed eyes, he keeps seeing his father falling down the stairs, his mother offering him an ice-cream, the kid at school that rubbed dog shit into his hair laughing at him, the ring popping on the last can of brew he drank, the foam squirting from the edges of the tab, frantically raising it to his lips, drinking, then his father...

His father. How old is Twitch? Young. Young enough that his father is still a giant, a God, infallible, love and judgment, all powerful. He smells of tobacco smoke and beer and sweat and love. Twitch is in his jim-jams, has Ted in his hand, and he's sitting on the stairs, scooting up backwards on his butt, laughing as his Dad crawls on all fours up after him, growling like a bear. He hears his mother's voice complaining, something about winding the boy up before bed, but Twitch is transported with a giggling fit, with glee and joy, scooting away from his father's grabbing hands, snatching his feet away *just in time*. When his father slips, the look of surprise on his face is so childlike, wide-eyed, comical, that Twitch laughs even harder, cackling helplessly as his father thud thud thuds down the steps, chin bouncing off each step, until Twitch sees his eyes roll back in their sockets, exposing dreadful whites. When his father hits the bottom of the stairs and crumples, he and his mother shriek in unison, in fear, and...

...and it's some endless summer holiday, and Twitch is sitting in the garden and Twitch is sad. He's sad because no-one wants to play with him. His only friend from school, Bradley, lives outside of town and his mum doesn't have a car, and no-one in the town likes him, and it's just a lovely summer day. He can hear other children cycle past in the street, some other kids walking and bouncing a ball and laughing. He hates them all, and their easy happiness, but mostly he hates himself – for his stupidity, his clumsiness, his inability to make anyone like him.

He sits in his garden and tries not to cry, to hold it all in, and it's like a big ball of glass in his stomach, expanding, pushing everything else out. When his mother touches his shoulder he just about jumps out of his skin, and she's smiling a cheer-up-you smile, and holding out an ice lolly. He stares at it, at her, and for a second a wave of unnameable feeling flows over him. He's too young for the concept of despair to really have any meaning. Nevertheless, this is his first taste.

The feeling threatens to engulf everything, batter down his self-control. He wants to knock the lolly out of her hand, slap her face, slap her silly, for a second he feels it so clearly it's like it's actually happening, and then the feeling breaks, and he takes the lolly and tries a smile. It feels horrible, fake on his face, but mum's smile widens, reaches her eyes, and oh well, he thinks, at least I cheered her up, and anyway, the lolly is nice, and then..

("... God will not be tested! Don't you get it? We'll be taken to the kingdom; you will burn, and for what? For proof of something that you'd get in your own time anyway?"

"I don't want it in my own time. I want it today. And I'm going to get it.")

...he hears the words, individually, but they slide off the smooth surface of what's left of his mind, leaving no impression, gone as soon as they are heard, and Andrew Jackson is pointing and laughing, the hard forced laugh that is not a laugh at all, but a fist, a ball of hate that he pummels Twitch with, just like he pummelled him in the street outside the school while they waited for the bus in the rain. Andrew Jackson, the only kid in Year 2 with a moustache and acne, with his torn jean jacket and Damage Inc. back-patch, and the smell of HubbaBubba and cigarette smoke. The smell of hate and anger and meanness and violence. Andrew Jackson is pointing and laughing, and the others are starting to join in as they realise what's happened, and Twitch stands there with the rain washing the dog shit down his face. He feels a lump of it roll down his cheek, can smell it where the turd was broken open, where the soft centre was exposed and then mashed into his scalp. It itches, maddeningly, but he can't scratch it. Can't get that shit under his nails, can't wash it from his hair, can only stand there, the shame burning and building until he thinks it must surely overwhelm him entirely. Remove him from the land of the living, strike him down, pull him into the earth. But of course it doesn't, it just burns and smoulders, and sinks, and when the bus arrives he lets them push past him without saying a word, the chant of "Shithead! Shithead!" fading but not eliminated as the doors close and the bus pulls away. Of course it's Andrew Jackson's face he sees last, in the rear window, face distorted in that hateful smile indistinguishable from fury, mouthing with exaggerated care "Shithead", and...

("...this all you've got, Preacher? I've read the book; you know. I'm not an idiot..."

"...No, no, that's not what I'm saying, I'm saying God told me..."

"...yes, why *is* he talking to you and not me? Given the situation, you'd have thought...")

...and it's Saturday night, and Twitch is back in his flat, good and drunk. He can feel the welcoming black fingers of oblivion tugging at the corner of his mind, promising the dreamless sleep of the cataclysmically bombed. The void in the eye of the storm, that blessed, perfect release. He can feel it growing, oozing across his mind like some benign tumour, sinking consciousness and all its attendant irritations, pains, misery. It's coming, and one more tin will do it nicely, and he has one left, so all is right with the world. He doesn't register the single tear that he sheds as he reaches into the flimsy blue carrier bag and pulls out the last tin, doesn't hear the single sob he gives as he pops the can, but his sluggish reflexes are good enough that when the foam comes, he gets the can to his lips and does not lose a drop.

Waste not.

He leans his head back against the wall and closes his eyes, shutting out the sight of the filthy bedroom, dimly lit by the sickly yellow glow of the outside streetlight (no power – Twitch's habit has long won the fight between putting a fiver on the 'leccy key or buying another few cans). Closing off the epic grime of the kitchen, with the racks of empty tins of food slowly mouldering. He closes his eyes to it all as he drinks, as he feels the darkness getting closer and the tears cut tracks through the dirt of his face, and all at once he's aware of a simple, basic truth: he doesn't want to wake up. He doesn't. He's spent, he's done, he doesn't want to do this anymore. He opens his eyes and regards the tin carefully, and right there, he decides. He's going to finish the can, and pass out. If he wakes up, he's done drinking; otherwise, he's just done. It's a comforting thought, a warming one. He hopes he doesn't wake up, but he knows, either way, this is his last tin of Brew. He's finished.

He drinks off a toast to his new understanding, and as he does so, the paper flyer that someone had chucked into his hat along with some change, that he'd transferred without thinking into the bag with the tins as he left the shop, floats into his field of vision, wrapped around the can, stuck there by the condensation. His eyes can make out the image of the cross imposed over a cartoon bomb, but not the words. Doesn't matter. Nothing matters. Nothing...

("...the Father...")

"No-one comes to the Father but through me? Right?"

"...Yes. But..."

"So fine, I'll take Jesus, that works fine for me. JESUS! I need to talk to you!"

"Son, it's not..")

And he's little, and his father is putting him to bed, crawling up the stairs, and he's laughing and laughing, so hard it's like he can't breathe, like he can't catch his breath, like he's drowning. His skin is crawling, like he's been dipped in dog shit, dog shit filled with worms and maggots that are crawling across his flesh, and as he opens his eyes he sees his hands caked in shit. He can smell it, and he sees the thin white worms crawling in it, on his flesh, and he springs to his feet, frantically rubbing his hands together, scratching, and he does not notice the pressure on his right arm, does not hear the sharp panicked whisper of the young man next to him, hears nothing beyond the noise of the raised voices on the stage and the pounding of his pulse, and he scratches, hard, and he bleeds, and he watches with horror as the worms start to crawl into the open wounds and burrow under his skin, and he screams now, tries to, but he is drowning, suffocating, and all that comes from his mouth is a high reedy sound, like a tap when the water's been cut off, and on the stage the young man and the preacher, locked in verbal combat, notice not a thing, and Twitch screams his silent scream again and again, each breath more shallow than the last, ragged now, desperate, and he sees the edges of his vision growing dim, and as consciousness retreats the last words he hears come from his side, as the young man next to him says loudly, "Um, Boss?"

Ecclesiastes

Chris is scared, terrified even, as the guy next to him deteriorates. He's terrified because he has no idea how the bomber will react, and he's suddenly acutely aware that these could be his last seconds on earth, and he's just not ready for it. But it's clear the guy is about to flake out big time, and that can't possibly be good, so he clears his throat and says,

"Um, Boss?"

It's apologetic, but it's also loud, and it carries all the way to the stage with ease. The bomber and preacher both pivot, in perfect unison, and even in this hyper-tense moment, Chris can't help but be amused on some level, *synchronised surprise!* The bomber meets his eyes, and Chris is pretty well paralysed by the intensity he sees there, thrown badly enough that he can't even remember for a second why he spoke up in the first place. There's a frozen moment of perfect agony where Chris wonders if he just killed everyone in the room and desperately tries to remember why the fuck he's standing up and talking.

Then Twitch comes to the rescue by just collapsing like a badly constructed tent.

Chris pulls back as Twitch slumps towards him, still terrified and jumpy from adrenaline, so Twitch's head rolls off his knee before hitting the ground. He lies there, like a broken doll thrown by an angry child, and Chris stares until a sense of sound and movement pulls his eyes back to the stage.

The bomber is sprinting down the aisle, right hand held high over his head, and Chris watches the tidal pull, the magnetic repulsion, as the people sat on aisle seats shrink back instinctively.

All except for Alex. She feels the pull, but stands her ground. This is new, and she wants to see the fuckhead as close as she can.

Especially because he's likely to have to make his way back to the stage, and when he does, the trigger will be on her side.

She makes ready.

Chris feels unable to move, that same paralysis effect rooting him to the spot like a fucking statue. When the bomber reaches him and slams past to get to the fallen man, Chris staggers backwards into the aisle, almost landing on his bum.

The benches are low, so Chris can see what follows very clearly. The bomber, right fist still in the air, is running his free hand over the head and face of the fallen man, then down to his hands, tracing the scratches. He looks up, out over the faces craned to look at him, anxious.

"Is anyone here a doctor?"

Silence.

"Nurse, First Aider? Anyone with any medical training at all?"

More silence, rolling, thick, oppressive. And Chris knows this has to be bullshit, there are what, seventy, eighty people in here and no first aider? Yeah, sure. Someone in here could do something, knows something, for damn sure. They're just sitting on their fucking thumbs. Chris feels a wave of disgust at that moment, palpable enough that he can taste it, and he actually thinks *you might as well blow this place. We're not worth it.*

The bomber has his back to Chris, so he can't read his face, but Chris guesses by the slump he sees in the bomber's shoulders that he's probably come to similar conclusions. The bomber half stands, turning towards Chris, then places a foot on the bench, and pushes it back violently, hard and fast enough to knock it over, as the other occupants leap to their feet to avoid getting in the way.

Having cleared some space, the bomber turns his attention back to the unconscious man, squatting to one side and looking at the grubby, pallid face with a fierce concern. He takes in the whole body, hesitant, then grabs the ankle of Twitch's left leg and starts to tug it, trying to straighten it out from the awkward angle it's fallen at, make him more comfortable.

That's the moment Twitch starts his fit.

His entire body heaves up, spasming, and his legs fly straight, pistoning down and out, sweeping the squatting bomber as efficiently as a martial artist. He goes flying backwards, hopelessly off balance, and for Chris that tumble seems to take about a million years. He sees the bomber falling back and away, still accelerating as he heads for the ground, and Chris has time to think *if he bangs his head hard enough, we all die right now,* has time to think *please God, I'm so sorry,* and then the bomber is on his back. His head does bounce off the floor, but the bulk of the device strapped to him means his neck has further to travel than it might have otherwise. He's already moving against the direction of travel, trying to sit up, so it's a pretty light smack, and his right arm remains perfectly straight and upright and his thumb does not slip and they are not all consumed in a ball of fire. There are gasps and shouts, and even a few screams, and Chris has managed to take a further two steps back without even thinking about it, but the bomber is already regaining his feet, moving back to the poor sod flopping like a fish on the floor. Chris's eyes are drawn back to this sight, and it's pretty horrible. The guy's heels are drumming on the ground, his head smacking against the hard wood floor again and again, arms flailing.

The bomber moves towards that banging head, hand out, as if to hold it down.

"No!"

The voice is frail sounding but remarkably deep. It comes from the old man who was sat in front of Chris. His wheezing is as bad as ever, maybe worse, but his watery blue eyes are alive and alert.

"Could hurt his neck. Here..."

The old man shrugs out of his heavy tweed jacket, slowly.

"...put this under his head."

The old man folds the cloth over twice and hands the makeshift pillow to the bomber. He takes it, making eye contact and nodding his thanks. The old man nods back, calm as you like.

Getting something under the head of someone having a seizure is no picnic, especially one handed, but the bomber manages it on the second attempt, and the dreadful smacking sound of skull on floor is replaced by a softer thudding. Chris realises the entire row in front of his has turned to look.

Every eye that can see is watching this scene.

Without looking around, he knows the same thing is happening in the other aisle as well. All minds bent to this spectacle. Even the priest is here, having followed the bomber at some point, his pale face a mask of concern.

All eyes are on the bomber, and the bomber is all about the poor guy on the ground, and the number of people looking at Chris is zero, and for the first time, Chris is aware of how close he's now standing to the entrance.

Or, you know, the exit.

He feels his heart rate kick up a little at the thought. Shit. Really close. How close? Six foot? Less? If he's going to leave, this is the moment. He doesn't want to die here today, he has realised, quite powerfully does not want to, despite the awful appeal of the bombers experiment. Could he do it? Would it work? The bomber is so much closer. Would the closed door, the walls, offer enough protection at that range? Could he get the door shut? Could he live with killing everyone else?

Would God forgive him?

"What are you thinking about? Son, what are you trying?"

It's the priest, and Chris feels like he's jumped about six feet in the air before his eyes and mind catch up with his freaking out central nervous system that just screams *caught! Caught! Caught!*

The priest is looking at the bomber, and there's uncertainty and a little anger in his voice, as well as the expected fear. Chris looks back at the bomber. He's on his knees, one leg on either side of Twitch's head, right arm still straight up in the air as if in some deranged salute. His left hand is nestled in the dirty hair of the still jerking head, and his eyes are closed. His brow is furrowed, but his face is otherwise flat. Chris feels a complicated wave of emotions as he watches, feelings he can't fully understand, but his overriding thought is that something is happening, something... powerful.

Without opening his eyes, the bomber says "A healing. I'm trying for a healing. I'm attempting to save this man's life, preacher. Pray for me to succeed, if you like, and if you can't or won't, just shut up."

There's another ripple through the crowd at this, felt as much as seen, part shuffle, part murmur, part intake of breath. Chris looks at the bomber, watches him as he gently rubs the scalp of the fallen man, eyes closed, clearly and completely focussed, and all thoughts of escape evaporate like a drop of water on a hot stove. He's drawn in completely, mesmerised by the drama in front of him.

The bomber inhales, slowly and deeply, once, twice. Then he draws in a fast, deep breath, and holds it, pushing against it, straining. His fingers splayed in the hair appear to press down, and his face gradually reddens as he increases the internal pressure. The moment builds. Then he lets the breath fly out, jerking his hand back at the same time in a tugging motion, as though pulling an invisible rope or wire. Immediately, the trembling becomes less acute, the drumming of arms and legs on the ground less insistent. A sigh comes from the crowd. Chris hears a click, realises it came from his dry attempt to swallow.

The bomber does not open his eyes, but returns his hand to Twitch's head, and begins the breathing again. The drumming of feet and hands against the floor has become an irregular tapping. This time when the bomber pulls, the reduction is less, but still, it seems clear to Chris that the bomber is having some effect.

Is this a miracle? Lord, is this a sign? THE sign?

Another round of breath, and it seems to Chris like he can feel the collective will of the congregation, all pulling for the bomber to succeed, for his patient to be well. When he makes that pulling gesture for the third time, the seizure fades almost entirely, only a mild tremor remaining in the hands, like a palsy.

The bomber opens his eyes, looking down into the face of the man he has tried to save. To Chris the concern and tenderness is unmistakable, and he lets out a breath he doesn't realise he's been holding. For the first time since the bomber made his move, Chris feels like they're going to be okay – that somehow, they're all going to make it out of here okay.

Maybe the plan isn't so crazy. Maybe God is with them after all.

Chris looks around, taking in the reactions of others. There's a lot of relief, even a few smiles, some mopped brows. Other faces are harder to read, still tight with tension and fear. The priest, now, he's a picture, and not a pretty one. To Chris' eyes, he looks appalled, disgusted. Upper lip curled in an unconscious snarl.

This could be trouble.

"Okay." Says the bomber, eyes not moving from the face of his patient. "Now, I think I need..."

And that's when Twitch wakes up – eyes burst open, bugged and staring, mouth gaping, stretched, back arching up from the floor like it's on fire, screaming an awful, throat-shredding yelp. Arms shot out to the side, hands like claws, tendons in the neck standing out like wires, screaming, screaming, then total collapse, the last of his breath leaving in a whispering sigh.

People freak out, jump back, flinch, there's some yelps and screams, and Chris feels his heart sink into his belly, because he's no kind of medic, but he's pretty sure this unfortunate young man just passed on, and sure enough, he sees the bomber check for a pulse in the neck, and the slump of his shoulders confirms it.

The hand on the neck moves back to the cheek, and the bombers eyes are closed again, screwed shut, brow furrowed, head trembling. For a minute, Chris, as spooked as he can remember ever feeling in his life, thinks maybe the bomber is trying for some outrageous Hail Mary, some Lazarus type thing. He has time enough to feel terror at the thought, blind horror, because what if he does it? What if he can bring another man back to life with his touch? What then?

But then he sees the tears running down the bomber's face, sees the tremble spread to his lips, his shoulders, and he feels a powerful wave of relief, mixed with a faintly nauseating shame.

He watches the bomber weep, silent sobs shaking his body, and his eyes are drawn as if by magnetism to the closed fist in the air. The hand is shaking a little but the thumb stays clamped down, knuckle white with the effort, and that's obviously not good, but it's better than the alternative.

The tableau holds for what feels like many minutes, the bomber sobbing, eyes closed, free hand stroking the cheek of the dead man. The bomber's tears run down his nose, drip onto the face of the body beneath until it looks like the corpse is crying too. *Baptized with salt* thinks Chris, and shudders.

The bomber opens his eyes, red and watery, hand still stroking the cheek of the dead man. "I'm sorry. I'm so sorry." His voice is cracked, choked.

Chris picks up on the movement and looks up in time to see the priest moving forward, arms raised. The look he'd seen before has passed, and what Chris sees now is compassion, concern. And something else, but Chris can't read it; he's too stoked, too frazzled.

"Son..." The priest reaches out, places his hand on the bomber's left shoulder. The bomber seems to flinch or freeze at the contact, momentarily, but then carries on breathing, the sobbing tapering off.

"Son. Please. Please."

The bomber does not raise his head, continues to stare into the face of the dead man.

"You have a good heart, son. I can see that now. You didn't want this to happen, did you? You didn't want this man to die. I don't think you want any of us to die, do you?"

There's a huge pause at this, and all Chris can seem to hear is the breathing of the two men – the bomber's, ragged and damp, slowing, the priest's calm and even.

"No."

"No. Of course you don't. Of course. You're just angry; that's all. You've been hurt son; I can see that, and you're angry about that pain. I want to tell you that I'm sorry about that. Truly I am."

The priest's grip tightens just a little on this last. Chris sees the fingers flex and observes the stiffening in the bomber's shoulders again.

"None of us want to hurt you, son. We want to help you. We love you."

The bomber's breath has been calming throughout this, but here it catches, and again Chris sees his lips tremble, a fresh tear squeeze out.

"I... I know you do."

Still raw, still wet. What the hell is going on inside that voice?

"Good. That's good." The priest actually smiles, and it looks warm and genuine.

"Then join us son, why don't you? Join us in fellowship, and renounce this path you're on."

Slowly, so slowly, the bomber raises his head, eyes moving from the body in front of him to the man standing over him, searching out the face, the eyes, of the priest. The priest waits for him and holds his gaze when their eyes do meet. Chris looks from one to the other, takes in the calm sincerity of the priest, and the sweaty, pale face of the bomber. To Chris, the bomber looks trapped, suspended between hope and despair, fear and love.

"Is it time to lay down the sword, preacher. Is that what you tell me?"

The priest nods. "It is, yes."

"And it's God's will that I do this?" Something – in his eyes, in his voice, Chris couldn't tell you what, but something – makes Chris' belly turn to lead. He feels a drawing back, like he's going to faint or something, and he wants to yell out, to scream at the priest to stop...

"It is, son."

...stop, stop now, there's still time, a chance, but you have to stop right now, or we're all going to die. Chris knows it, he feels it, but he's paralysed by fear, by the forces at work between these two men, he's trapped in a nightmare and he cannot speak, cannot act...

"God has told me to tell you this. To lay down your sword, and let Him into your heart. Will you do it?"

The bomber takes a deep breath, holds it. On the

exhale, he brings his left arm down slowly, still stiff-arm straight, until the fist holding the trigger rests on the priest's shoulder. At the same time, he rises from his crouch, one of his knees cracking loud enough to make Chris flinch.

They hold it for a second, looking into each others' eyes. *Like soldiers*, Chris thinks, and he is so afraid now. The bomber takes a half step back and reaches his right hand up his left sleeve, and there's a ripple of panic, people staggering away from the bomber. Chris takes two quick steps back, not thinking, and feels his heels hit something solid.

Holy shit. The door, or the wall?

Doesn't matter. He can't look away. Can't take his eyes off the bomber. If he's about to die, so be it. The bomber struggles for a second with his sleeve, and the priest's eyes narrow, a half flinch, and then the bomber pulls his right fist from his arm, revealing the blade in a clean drawing motion. As it slides out smoothly, Chris notices his arm bend for the first time, and now he understands the theatrical stiff-arm, and as he thinks this, even in his terror mentally slapping his own forehead, the two foot blade is out and the priest finally sees what lies beneath the bomber's eyes. Too late, he tries to move backwards and turn all at once and manages neither, feet tangling together. He staggers back, swaying on his centre of gravity, overcorrects, and his body is still moving forwards, back towards the bomber, when the blade enters his belly.

The bomber has actually crouched and turned before plunging, like a corkscrew. The blade enters the priest low in the stomach, on an inexorable upward trajectory, driven hard and fast and true. Chris sees the blood bloom immediately on the priest's shirt, and observes with a detached air the blade pass into the priest's body until the hilt, and the bomber's fist, rest against the red stain.

The priest opens his mouth, makes a single choking noise which turns into a gargle as blood first drools then erupts from his open mouth. Chris sees the priest's legs give way, and the bomber falls to his knees in perfect sync, like ballet, still holding the metal in place. The priest is looking up, still gargling and rattling his death, arms low and spread as if in supplication, fingers trembling. Then the head slowly lowers, and Chris sees those eyes meet the gaze of his killer one final time, before the pupils dilate, and the head drops completely.

The bomber leans forward, touches his forehead briefly to the priest's, then uses his shoulder to push the body off of the sword, grunting with the effort. It takes a few seconds, but the blade is finally withdrawn, the priest's body slumping to one side, blood flowing from the entry wound, pooling on the wooden floor.

The room is silent. All Chris can hear is breathing – his own, the others, the bomber. The priest lays there and bleeds, from his mouth and belly, and the bomber kneels, looking down. No-one moves, no-one says a word.

Chris is suddenly aware of a pressure in the small of his back, and he realises he's leaning against the door handle.

It's a big pull handle, brass effect, fire door with a weighted automatic closer. Chris sees it in his mind as surely as if he's looking at it, perfect recall from when he walked into here, a million years ago – and did it make any noise when it opened, when it shut? It did not. He keeps his head stock still, and allows his eyes to do the walking.

No-one is looking at him at all, not even close. All eyes are on the slaughter, and Chris realises this is it.

This is it.

He allows himself one more breath to think about it, but nothing changes. He still doesn't want to die here.

It feels to Chris like it's the very second *before* he starts to reach for the door that the bomber's head snaps up, and his eyes root Chris to the spot like a bug under a pin.

The bomber is still on his knees, the blood now darkening the knees of his trousers, and he raises his reddened fist and points the blade right at Chris. Chris has time to see the spray of blood that comes off the blade as he does this. Has time to see a drop, big and fat and pregnant, roll and drip off the point, splashing on the ground.

"If you want to go, go. But do it now."

Chris pants, a cornered animal, but he makes no effort to move. He can't. He can't. He just fucking can't. The moment holds; the bomber pointing, eyes on Chris but performing just the same, thinks Chris, letting the whole room know for sure who's in charge now. And is it just a game? Could Chris call his bluff?

Too late.

"I need you all to understand what will happen if you lie to me. If you mistake the voice of your mind for the voice of God. You will be cast down. Do you see that now?"

Chris sees nods out of the corner of his eyes.

The bomber pulls himself back to his feet, and Chris could swear he looks taller, somehow. He tries to reconcile the expression he sees now with the crying man of a few long minutes ago, and he can't do it. There's something happening here...

And is this the mask, or was the other?

We're dead, thinks Chris. *I'm dead.*

The blade is still pointing at him, and now it flicks to the overturned bench, and Chris hears the quiet rat-a-tat-tat as another blood splatter hits the floor. Chris feels his flinch, and sees a flicker of what has to be amusement on the bomber's face – something that happens at the corner of his eyes and then is gone.

"Pick up the bench. Put it back."

At first Chris thinks he won't be able to move. That he'll just stand there frozen until the bomber loses patience and guts him like a pig, but, of course, this isn't *that* kind of nightmare. Now that it's too late, he finds his limbs respond to his commands just fine, thanks, and he does as he's told.

The blade points at the corpse of the young man, face still wet with the tears of the killer.

"Move him into the aisle, would you? Lay him next to the preacher."

The tone is calm, conversational, perfectly in control, and Chris feels a surge of hatred that he'd never suspected was in him. It washes in fast and then fades, leaving a sick churning in his gut and a metallic taste in his throat. He bends over the dead man, and hooks his armpits; head turned to one side, so he doesn't have to look at that slack, damp face. He tries to ignore the smell, body odour like rotting bin bags mixed with the unmistakeable stench of fresh shit. The body is heavy, *dead weight, haha*, and it's an awkward angle, especially with his own neck twisting away to avoid looking, but fear is a powerful motivator, and Chris manages to drag the body out into the aisle without dropping him.

As he lays the body down, he staggers back a step, then shakily returns to his seat. Once there, he turns and watches as the killer goes back on his knees and kisses the forehead of the dead man, eyes shut.

Then he stands and does a slow turn, pointing at the entire room with his blade. Marking them. Then it points at the big clock, impossibly reading 10:47, as if all that has passed could possibly have occurred in ten minutes, as opposed to the five point four years Chris is sure he's just lived through.

"The preacher was a dead end. More prayer, I think. Take a knee, if that's what works for you. Either way, do what you've got to do, but do it quietly. Pray now."

The blade dips to the floor. The bomber stands in the aisle, back to the stage, the two bodies side by side, the blood from the priest oozing under the corpse of the young man. Chris hears nothing but the breathing of the survivors.

The killer turns and strides back down the aisle towards the stage. Chris lowers his head and closes his eyes.

Psalms (II)

Alex is breathing hard. She doesn't know it, but her nostrils are flaring, and her pupils are dilated.

She was ready five minutes ago. Five minutes ago, she had it all so clear she could picture it. The dickhead would walk back up the aisle towards the stage, arm either straight out or straight up, and when he passed Alex, she'd just grab his fist in both her hands and fucking crush his thumb against the button. Tangle his legs, make him fall and land on top of him, yell "Get him! Get him!" She knows the sax player will be there because she's been in near constant contact with him since the dickhead left the stage. Eyes flicking, facial twitches, significant head inclinations – it's been a regular Jane Austen novel. She's gonna jump this dickless wonder on his way back to the stage, and Mr. Sax player, all six lovely tough feet of him, is gonna be there in about four seconds even if nobody else grows a pair, and then the party is over, hasta la vista baby, book him, Danno.

But that was five minutes ago. A lifetime has passed since then. Now the scumbag is walking back down the aisle towards her with a fucking *sword* still dripping blood in his right hand, and the left hand, the one with the switch, the one she was going to grab, is swaying by his hip as he strides towards the stage, and she has maybe three seconds to make a decision, and she can feel her hands trembling but that's not going to stop her, fuck that, this is still her best shot, he has to be stopped. She tries not to think about the sword. About whether or not it'll hurt. About if she can avoid it for long enough for her knight to arrive. She glances over, quickly, makes eye contact one last time, set, and that's when the sax player shakes his head, just once.

Mike sees the fury, the disbelief in the girl's face, and for a horrible moment, he thinks maybe she's going to just go anyway, but she doesn't. She holds her place, and the boy walks past her with no idea how close he came, and Mike permits himself a long, slow exhale. It's going to be okay. The moment of maximum danger has passed. God is with him, with them. In God, he trusts.

He meets her gaze again, once the boy retakes the stage, and her lips are a thin line, her eyes blazing, and he bobs his head slightly. His right eyebrow flickers. He twitches his sax with his arm, as though shifting the weight, and looks at the sword, then back at the girl. She swallows hard, still angry, but finally nods back.

Good.

Mike takes in the scene. The bodies in the aisle, side by side, the blood pooling out, dark against the wooden flooring. There's a lot of pale faces out there, a lot of dark rings under eyes. Some tears too, people trying to cry quietly, couples comforting each other as best they can.

He takes in the front row. Sees the two wheelchairs, the parent with the boy, the girl that spoke up, head lowered now in prayer or fear, and the couples lined up on his side. In particular, he takes in the pregnant woman. He knows her; at least, he's seen her before, at the born again services, knows her to say hello to.

Her head is lowered, her husband's arm around her, neither of them looking up, and Mike takes them in. He sees her heightened breathing, the hunched shoulders. He wonders how long she has left to run.

Mike clasps his hands in front of him and lowers his head. He waits. For God.

Emma's not doing so good.

She's sweating too much, for one. No, perspiring, ladies perspire, she tries to focus on that but it doesn't help, because she's blinking well sweating, that's all. Her belly is rolling, like there are stones in there, and she's pretty sure the cramps she's feeling are not indigestion.

She's pretty sure they're contractions.

Peter has his hands on her shoulders, is rubbing them and breathing calming words into her ear, a rolling prayer, "Lord Jesus help us. Lord Jesus we thank you for the life you have entrusted to us. Lord God help us to be strong. Lord Jesus help us to stand in your light. Lord God help us to do your will."

On and on, a mantra of hope, of supplication. It's like cold water on third-degree burns; it helps, but not enough. Dear Lord not enough, because her baby is coming now, she's sure of it. She's tried to ignore it and tried to fight it and begged for it not to happen but now it's happening, and oh dear Lord she is so afraid now, so very, very afraid.

Another wave of cramps come, more powerful than the last, and she can't help the low moan that escapes her lips, and Peter stiffens, stops rubbing momentarily, and she knows that he knows.

What are they going to do?

On the other side of the aisle, Deborah hears that moan, like the lowing of a hungry calf. She does not look around, does not raise her head. Her frustration has turned to fury that she now experiences as a physical thing, no longer hot but a cold ball of lead in her gut. Deborah has decided to kill this young man. She doesn't know how, no clue, but she has promised herself that she will.

It's not the death of the priest, exactly – Deborah has suffered enough heartache and false hope at the hands of such men that tears would be hypocritical. No, it's the callousness with which it was done that upsets her. The calculated nature of it.

The theatre.

You're no better than him. He may have claimed hope, and you fear, but I think it's just the same bullshit either way. You took him to make a point to the rest of us. We're all just pawns to you.

Deborah has decided her days as a pawn are over. She's been pushed around from place to place, according to the designs of others, for long enough. God is real, and He's not going to do a damn thing about this horror show. He never does. The only thing they have is His only gift – free will. The bomber has it. So does she.

She will use it. She will end him.

The woman moans again, and Deborah allows the moan into her mind, alongside the twitching next to her, the whimpering sniffling she can hear behind her. She absorbs it, building her disgust, her belly churning, becoming hard.

She feels that cold ball of metal in her stomach, turns it, spinning, and imagines it flowing, liquid, into her legs, creating a metal skeleton for her lower body. She pictures it; she feels it. Her mind is so captivated by the image, by the idea, that she doesn't notice that her left big toe has, for the first time in seven years, twitched.

Three rows behind Deborah, seated on the end of the bench, next to the wall, **Katie** is feeling numb. Faint. She is haunted by the bloody death of the priest. She sees it again and again. The back of his head tilting back. The blood spray. The sound of his body slumping to the floor, like a heavy roll of carpet dropped on hard ground.

She sees it, eyes open, eyes closed. Over and over. He

grunts; he falls. The lunatic falls with him, and she sees his face over the head of the priest. His awful blank eyes.

He means to kill them all, and she cannot see how this will not come to pass. She tries to pray, to pray for humility or whatever, to pray that she can be brave, to pray that she will go to heaven. To pray that it won't hurt too much.

That her parents will forgive her. Their stubborn daughter, determined to shake up their cozy Church of England lives by going to the service that promised a revolution in the church. That they will not blame each other for letting her go. Will not be too sad for too long.

She looks to her right, at the sweaty bald man who'd been praying so earnestly when the band was playing. A little too earnestly for her taste, like he was trying too hard – hand in the air, eyes tight shut, swaying. He looked so miserable, needy. It's worse now. He's sat on the bench, head in his hands, shoulders hunched. Katie can't tell for sure, but she thinks he may be crying. She thinks about trying to comfort him, put an arm round him, but he still looks sweaty and gross, and besides, she's too afraid to move.

Instead, she tries to pray. But her mind will not move away from the murder and the maniac.

Shock fractures time the same way it fractures thoughts. Reflections become jagged; perception distorted. The seconds take hours now, the hours seconds. So many minds now frantic rats running on wheels that turn nothing, produce nothing but elevated heart rates and sweat and more fear - vicious circles turning in terrified minds. The clock no longer feels like any kind of objective measure – it feels like an abstraction, a lie. The lie we all tell ourselves to preserve a sense of order in the raw chaos of true reality. So it means little to most of the congregation that the clock reads 11:56 when a combination of the pain of the contraction and the accompanying blood pressure dip causes Emma to first cry out, and then collapse.

Isaiah

"... **y** cushions, any..."

Thud. Thud.

"...under her head, elevate her..."

Thud. Thud.

"...Emma? Emma?"

Peter. She latches onto his voice, swims toward it, through the roaring blackness.

"Emma? Squeeze my hand, sweetheart."

So tender. He only calls her that when she's sick. When she's...

"Squeeze my hand."

She tries, her hand flickers, and she feels his sigh on her face.

"Good job, sweetheart. Good job. Jesus, we ask you..."

Fade out again. Each breath feels like wind blowing in and out the mouth of a dark, hot cave. It surrounds her, the booming of her heart like a drum. Gradually, she becomes aware of pink light, a glow. She swims towards it again, trying to surface.

"...thank you for each other, for the blessing of our union, and Lord we ask..."

She sways back again, tidal currents pulling her back from the voice, from the light. Suddenly there's a stabbing pain in her stomach, and she feels a surge of panic, terror, and she surfaces all at once, eyes flying open, hand clamping around her husband's in a death grip because she is dying, she's just been stabbed in the stomach, that evil monster has killed her, killed her baby, he's standing over her with that sword, the feeling is so vivid, so *sure*, that even after the signal from her eyes is telling her that it's not so, that the space above her is empty save the concerned face of Peter at her right side, part of her still believes it. Then the pain shifts, turns and subsides, just another contraction, *thank you God, thank you.*

She shifts her head slightly, eyes focussing on Peter's caring, concerned face. His brown eyes behind the half-moon glasses. So handsome, her husband. Such a good man. She feels a surge of love and pride, lifts her hand from his and touches his cheek, softly.

"I'm okay, darling. I'm okay."

"Of course you are." He smiles then; not just handsome, beautiful, and she follows the path of a lone tear as it escapes the corner of his eye, running down his cheek.

"Yes. But Peter..."

Her throat is dry; it clicks as she swallows, tries again.

"... I think I'm having a baby."

She smiles and feels her own eyes tearing up in unison with his, and her laugh comes out as a sob. His jaw trembles, comes back under control, but the tears are flowing freely now, and his return smile looks painful. She feels the love, the comfort he is trying to give her, and she takes from it gratefully, hungrily, her hand dropping from his face, lacing her fingers with his.

"It's okay. It's going to be okay. This is God's plan for us."

He tries to reply, cannot. Nods too fast, shakily.

She rolls her eyes left and right, as far as she can, trying to get a sense of where she is. She can make out the edge of the stage behind Pete, an empty bench to her right. Her back reports solid floor underneath, but her head is resting on something softer.

Her eyes return to Peter's face. His cheeks are wet, but

he's more in control. Good. She needs him strong, needs to lean on him and his strength so that she can be strong too.

"Can I get you anything? Anything you need?"

She considers the question carefully, feeling hundreds of potential answers that would open up the well of despair or fury, refusing them all, seeking out the righteous path, the road to salvation.

"Some water would be good, if there is any. I'm thirsty."

Peter looks up at the stage. She can tell by his expression who he's looking at, and she turns her mind away, thinks only of the child in her belly and the need to breathe slow and deep and even. Just a blood pressure dip, it can happen with the contractions, they'd told her that, perfectly normal, nothing to worry about. Perfectly normal. The words and the breathing exercises she's practised all this time do their work, and she tries to find calm...

"Does anyone have any water? This woman is in labour; she needs a drink."

The voice is loud and clear, and she shudders, and inside her mind the walls tremble, become thin, and she can see the shape of him through them, the silhouette, blade in one hand, button in the other, and she hears movement from a long way away, but it feels so distant, his shadow grows and grows, blotting out the light, all light, she feels her breathing increase, her heart start to gallop, the edges are closing in, the tide is rising again, pulling her out and away, the shadow claiming all, and then there's her husband's arm under her head, gently lifting the bottle to her lips, and she takes a sip of blessedly cool water. It coats her throat with a blue line, swims into her belly, and she comes back to herself, to Peter, his loving face looking down at her.

"Better?"

She nods.

"More?"

"In a minute."

She allows her heart to slow, luxuriates in the feeling of Peter's hand on her brow, the soothing gentle stroking. She closes her eyes for a second, smiles.

"That feels good."

She opens them again, sees his answering smile, feels the blessing of his love. She's going to be okay. *They're* going to be okay. If it's God's plan that she deliver her child in a church, so be it. It's even fitting, in a way.

"Peter?"

"Yes love?"

"Save some of the water, will you? Just a bit. I might not remember later."

"Why?"

She smiles, and its warmth lights up her whole face.

"In case we need to do a baptism."

She watches understanding cross his face, sees the fight between love and fear, and is exulted as love wins, and he grins at her.

"God's will?"

"God's will." She reaches for his hand, still holding the bottle, and gently squeezes it. "I love you so much, Peter. So much."

"I love you too."

"Good. Can I have another sip of water, please?"

"Yes, of course."

He lifts her head again, she takes one sip, then a second, and the next contraction hits just as she's swallowing, and her teeth click together as she clenches her jaw, because this is starting to hurt now, really hurt. She feels all her muscles down there cramping, squeezing, tighter than she would ever have thought possible. Her windpipe burns with misdirected water, and she half coughs, half gags. She tries to hold her breath to stop from coughing more, but the cramps make it impossible, and she coughs again, each cough sending an answering stab to her stomach, and the pain and the cramp and the rawness of her throat combine in a horrible surge, and she turns her head sideways and retches, feeling the blood force into her face and her eyes bulge as the water comes back up, splashing on the floor. She tears another breath in, convinced she's going to do it again, but the cramp in her stomach begins to relax again. She manages to switch to her nose, panting like a dog, willing her stomach back under control, her throat to stop burning, and little by little, inch by inch, they do.

Both her hands are clamped around Peter's now, and it's an effort to get her fingers to relax, but she does it and looks back up at him. She sees love and concern, but little fear. Good deal. This is going to be hard, she thinks, very hard indeed, but she knows that her husband has steel in his heart as well as love. She wills that steel to manifest now, to meld with his faith and his love for her, because she's going to need every ounce of his calm strength to keep the world at bay, and let her focus on what she needs to do, on bringing this child into the world.

Because the child is coming, and she's pretty sure her baby is going to arrive in this building, not the hospital bed they'd planned for. *If that's your will Lord, let it be done, but let my man stay strong, Lord, and let me do what I need to do.*

"Peter."

Her voice is harsh, ragged from the vomiting, but clear.

"Yes, love."

"I'm going to need your help. I need to take my pants off."

He swallows, blinks hard once. Nods.

"Can you stand?"

She considers the question carefully. Could she stand? She's pretty sure she could if there were a... if she had to, but after careful consideration, she decides she'd rather not, actually. For one thing, if she has another contraction while she's on her feet, she might pass out and fall again, which would be bad for the baby. For another, she thinks the less she moves right now, the better. She will have this baby in this church, on this floor, if she has to. If it is God's will. However, if it's her choice, she'd just as soon do it in a hospital bed, and her best chance for that is to do as little as possible to help this process along. So...

"I don't think so, no. I'm worried I might pass out. Can you...?"

"Of course."

He moves, and his hands slide up under her skirt, tracing the shape of her thighs until they reach her hips. He has a nasty tendency to tickle her inadvertently sometimes, when he's touching these areas, but either his technique or the circumstances prevent this from happening, blessedly. He slides his thumbs under the elastic, looking at her questioningly, and she nods and lifts her hips, and he smoothly slides her pants down.

The moment triggers a memory that is almost impossibly vivid. She sees them inside the doorway of their honeymoon suite, returning from a very fine evening meal, falling into each other's arms, young and drunk and glowing with love and lust, a sudden embrace, open-mouthed kissing, bodies so hungry for each other reaching and grasping, pulling at clothes, and his hands had slid up her skirt just like that, hooked and pulled off the elastic as she'd unbuckled his belt, tugged open his zipper, reached into his pants and pulled him out, towards, and into her, he just stepping into her welcoming body, pulling him close and in and up, and ah, the joy, the pleasure, the rightness, the love.

The moment, the vision, has come and gone before her pants leave her ankles, and she is left with the glow of the memory, the feeling of certainty that she has a part and a place in the world, and that feeling of marvel and surprise that has never left her, that she has found him, her match, her other half. That God had provided this wonderful man for her to love.

"Peter? Can you come here, please?"

He kneels at her side, brings his face over hers, and she threads her hand through his hair and brings his lips to hers. The kiss is warm and full, loving but not sexual. As they break, he looks back at her, clearly delighted, smiling.

"I love you. No matter what. We're going to be okay. No matter what. Do you understand?"

He nods.

"Good. Now..."

And that's when the blade strikes the ground next to her.

She sees the sharpness of it, up close, even through the blackening blood that coats it, congealing like some awful wound that cannot heal. As though the sword itself were bleeding.

Hunched behind it, she sees the black jeans of the killer, his scuffed boots. Her eyes are drawn upwards, across that belt of wires and pale blocks. It seems to her that it radiates malevolence, that she can feel an awful destructive force just begging to be released, to explode and burn and rip apart everything, and her eyes go up to the clean shaven chin, the scraggly dark hair, the thin lips, pale pink against an even paler skin, that odd, hooked nose, those piercing blue eyes under that heavy brow, she sees him, and she feels the love and memory of love draining away, being drawn within, flooded out by fear, panic, despair, and she does not want to face this man, does not want to hear his voice, but she has no choice, because here he is, and he clearly means to speak.

Dear Lord, protect me now. Dear God protect my child. My God, please...

A tongue darts out and licks both lips.

"I'm so sorry about this. Is there anything we can do to make you more comfortable?"

Amos

She makes herself breathe slow and deep.

"You could let my husband and I go, that would certainly make me feel more comfortable."

She hates the slight tremble she hears in her voice, the vulnerability robbing her words of their calm, subverting her intention.

His face twitches, in either humour or discomfort.

"I can't. Really."

"Yes, yes you bloody can!"

She's surprised by her anger, delighted by how it overrides the fear.

This time the wince is unmistakable.

"I understand how you feel, but..."

The laughter rips out of her throat, harsh and angry, shocking both of them, she thinks.

"Excuse me! You... you understand how I feel? Given birth a lot, have you? While having your life, and the life of your husband and child threatened? While..."

His face crumbles, and it's like a mask settles in its place as he begins to stand back up. She grabs his flapping jacket and pulls him back down. Shocked, overwhelmed by the surge of anger she now feels, stronger and hotter than she can ever remember experiencing. From a distance she hears gasps and at least one yell of fear, and somewhere deep in her mind a calm voice is asking if she's trying to get herself and everyone else killed, but she's too flipping angry to hear that voice, to acknowledge it, so she yanks on the fist-full of shiny black fabric, delighting in the look of surprise on his face, exulting at his stagger as he wobbles, almost falls, on his way back to the squat.

Lord, why does it feel so good to scare this man?

"...I'm not finished! You don't have the first idea, the tiniest inkling of what we are going through right now. If you did, you'd do the honourable thing and let us all go now."

His face is working again, and she sees emotions rippling, churning.

"I..."

"God's going to crush you like an insect, you know that? Like a woodlouse. Now or later, as to His will. He is Almighty. You? You're just a vile child with a magnifying glass, burning for the fun of it. Well, we are real people, as real as you, we feel pain, and if you go through with this, you will burn for eternity. For my child, if nothing else, you will burn!"

As soon as she mentions God she sees his face change, first becoming still, then hardening, knows she's not reaching him, is driving him further away, but does she not care, cannot stop.

"You're a believer?"

The calmness, the coldness with which he asks, cuts through her rage, shortens her breath. She feels her mind return to the bloody blade, so close to her body. The face of a killer that she can no longer read. The certainty drains away with the fury, and behind it the panic scrabbles and scratches at her mind.

"I..."

She falters, wondering if the truth will damn her, will kill her and hers. But she's come too far, said too much already. *Okay Lord. If it's your will, it's your will. Forever in your arms, Lord.*

Please help me to be unafraid.

"..Yes, I am."

He leans forwards, his eyes now like chips of ice, flat but sparkling with some kind of intelligence. She does not want to look. She does not dare to look away.

"Even now?"

She sees the blade move in her peripheral vision, the red shape lift like rain, return.

She swallows, mouth dry again.

"Yes, even now."

He nods, processing, wheels spinning.

"And have you been praying?"

"I have, yes. For myself, for our child, for my husband. For all of us."

"All of us? Even the woodlouse?"

His tone is light, conversational, but she hears an edge of anger, buried deep but lurking, a razor blade hidden beneath the skin of an apple.

"I... Yes. Even you. I have prayed for you to see the wrong in what you are doing, to feel God's love, to turn away from this path."

Another single nod.

"Thank you for that."

It surprises her, somehow, throws her. She sees his eyes mist up for a moment, before clearing.

"Can I ask you something? As a believer?"

She frowns, shakes her head, exasperation mixing with dread, the cocktail making her feel nauseous. Who is he, to ask her permission at the point of a blade? Why does he talk like they're just having a conversation in the street?

"What choice do I have?"

He starts back at that, seeming genuinely surprised, even hurt. She feels the exasperation and fear both double down, because she thinks that somehow, in his mind, this is a choice, some kind of... not game, but exercise, some kind of extreme theatre. She thinks that he does believe what he says, that he is trying to talk to God, that he sees them all not as victims of some hideous crime, but as participants in his cause. The dissonance troubles him, far more than beating a crippled girl or thrusting a sword into the stomach of the preacher bothered him. She feels her terror rise in earnest at this revelation, because it means the side of this man's mind is like solid ice, and they can scrabble and shout and bang against it, see through it, but never penetrate, never move him, and that means...

It means causing the dissonance is very dangerous, because yes, enough of it might make the ice shatter, but it might just set him off instead. He means what he is saying, she knows that, believes it as strongly as she believes anything, and she curses her own anger, her flare of temper, and prays she hasn't killed them all.

Please, God, Please.

"...choice. That's why I'm asking."

She's missed the start through the sudden pounding of blood in her ears. She feels flushed, hot. She takes his meaning, even so.

"Okay, okay. Ask."

He hesitates, nervous - again his face moves. Emotions clashing, she thinks.

"Has he spoken to you? Have you heard God's voice?"

She is aware of the blade again, aware of the warning this man gave after he killed the preacher, she considers long and hard whether or not a lie makes sense. The problem is not the first lie, she thinks, but all the ones that will have to follow, the different version of her life she might have to articulate. Could she do it without slipping, distracted as she is? And if she were to slip, what would he do then?

No. Tell the truth and shame the devil.

"Yes, I have. Often, when I pray, I've asked questions, for guidance, and God has told me the path I need to take."

He leans in, fascinated. He looks young, suddenly, frighteningly young.

"Can you... would you mind sharing an example?"

She thinks, but really there's only one example. The

story she always tells.

"Well, I prayed about Peter. My husband."

She raises her hand without looking in his direction. Feels him take it in his own, the touch and shape instantly familiar, comforting.

"When I first met Peter, at church... well, I didn't know quite what to make of him. I liked him and enjoyed his company, but... we had differences. I worried. About long term compatibility, and other things."

She's told the story so many times; the words are as familiar and comfortable as an old winter coat. Yet in this telling, she feels herself drawn back into the place the words describe, reliving the feelings.

"He'd made it clear that he took me very seriously, that he was devoted to me. He... declared an interest, I suppose you could say. And then we had a row – quite a bad one, it seemed at the time – and I took myself off and found a quiet spot. And I prayed."

She closes her eyes here, giving herself over to the memory.

"And I said 'Lord, tell me what I am to do about this man. I am lost, Lord, tell me the way forward. I would know your will, and be your vessel.' And I stayed very calm, and very still, and finally I heard His voice. And He said 'Peter is a good man. If you love him well, you will be well loved in return'."

She takes a deep breath, and it shudders a little on the exhale. She doesn't cry, doesn't sob, but her throat is tight, achy.

She opens her eyes and sees the killer staring at her, transfixed. For a few seconds, neither speaks. Then he asks

"And this is Peter?"

She nods, unaware that Peter is also nodding in sync.

"And are you well loved?"

"I am. The Lord keeps his promises, I believe. And so does Peter."

The young man nods again, smiles, and it lights up his

face. For a second, she thinks maybe everything will be okay after all.

"It's a good story. May I ask your name?"

"I'm Emma."

"Well met, Emma."

He goes quiet for a second, and she can see he's hesitating, thinking.

"I... Emma, can I ask something else?"

She feels another flair of anger at this, at his perverse sham of permission, but this time she is ready for it, holds it in check.

"Yes."

"What does He sound like? When He talks to you, what does His voice sound like?"

Again she feels possibilities turning in this moment, questions behind the question, the fear of a wrong answer, the futility of lying, and again she comes back to the simplest answer: the truth.

"He sounds... quiet. He doesn't shout. I have to get very calm and relaxed. I really have to listen. He whispers. The words... I hear them in my heart. I know how that sounds, but it's the truth. I hear His words in my heart, and they feel like love."

The young man sighs at this, a ragged sound. He suddenly looks like he's on the edge of tears.

"And... has He spoken to you, since..."

He waves the arm with the detonator, taking in the scene. She feels a ball of ice in her abdomen at that, feels her skin pop with sweat.

"No. No. I can't... I can't get calm enough to hear him."

She makes eye contact, wanting him to hear this next, wanting him to feel it.

"I'm too afraid."

She keeps her voice level by sheer will, but can do nothing about the tear that escapes the corner of her eye. So be it. Tell the truth. She feels Peter squeeze her hand, squeezes back in gratitude.

The young man lowers his head and closes his eyes. She's not entirely unsurprised to see that he is crying too, tears rolling down to the end of his nose, dripping onto her shirt. Then he starts to moan, a low sound, like a fog horn. The moan lasts a long time, a single held note becoming quavery as his breath expires. His whole frame begins to shudder, and she stares with paralysed terror at the arm holding the detonator, the fist holding all their lives in the balance, trembling and twitching, and she sends up a sudden prayer as a yell in her mind but she hears nothing back, and instead she raises her free hand, and hesitantly strokes the face of her killer.

His response is immediate, violent. He leaps back, up and away, landing on his backside, sliding across the polished stage, with a yelp like a sleeping dog kicked awake. The sound is horrible, terrified. Trapped.

He scrabbles backwards, then finds his feet. Lifting his head, he draws a huge breath, then yells to the ceiling, cords in his neck standing rigid like wires under his skin, face turning red, voice ripping with the force of it, like something leaving his body, arms rigid at each side, the sword and the detonator, *justice corrupted* she thinks, mind spinning, reeling, and she pulls Peter closer, an act of animal comfort, sure this is the end, and that's when her next contraction hits, triggered prematurely by the chemicals flying into her bloodstream as a result of her terror, her body hearing the message from the brain, *time is short, make hay, make hay,* and it's too soon and too big and she cries out in surprise and pain, the grip and clench enormous, body trying frantically to deliver the impossible, and ah God the agony, it blots out everything else, her jaw clamps and her hand crushes and she's making her own animal moaning sound now, the parallel with the killer lost to her, along with all higher brain function, down here is only pain and fear and the push.

She tries not to, but might as well try and push away

the ground beneath her back and fly. She strains, and feels something move, slide into place, *something is happening, oh God, something is happening,* but then the surge begins to abate, her muscles start to unlock, her breath returns to her. She feels the sweat running down her face, slicking her palms, feels Peter's poor hand, crushed into her own. She pants, each breath coming a little smoother, a little calmer. The contraction has passed, *thank you Lord,* the pain is lesser, *thank you God, please Lord please God don't make me have this child here.* She makes eye contact with Peter, and God bless him he's there, eyes seeking out hers, concerned, you bet, but with her all the way, *thank you God, thank you for this good man.*

She knows now, knows it's for real, knows she is having this baby, and soon. She also understands at the raw, gut- level that fear will only force things to happen quicker, her body reacting to the danger by trying to save the child. Knows too that if the child comes too quickly, if her own terror drives the process, the coming of her baby might kill her. Might kill them both.

Don't think about it. Don't think about the man with the bomb and the blade. Don't think about the yelling, the ranting from the stage, the voice spitting out words like they taste bad, hurling them into the room. *Don't think of elephants,* she thinks grimly, remembering the childhood game her brother would torment her with on long car journeys. *Don't think of elephants,* and it actually works, for a moment, all she can think of is elephants. She sees Dumbo, surrounded by the dancing pink elephants, freaking out, and it calms her, enough to regain eye contact with Peter, hold his gaze.

"Peter."

"Yes, love?"

So calm. So strong for her. She chokes back a sob.

"Help me to not be scared, will you? I need to not be scared."

He turns pale, his lips tighten, and for a terrible

moment, she sees the terror in his own mind. The roaring fear of her being hurt, of what is to come, the birth and his own powerlessness. She sees these storms cross his face, and she has time to feel an icicle of panic in her chest, and a groaning feeling in her mind, as though something foundational has come under massive strain.

Then the clouds pass, and Peter smiles his brilliant smile. His free hand strokes her brow, smoothing her damp hair back against her scalp.

"Dear Lord, we thank you for the gift of our child. Lord Jesus we pray in your name for a safe delivery. Most Holy God we trust ourselves to your will, we..."

The words wash over her, soothing. She feels the ice melt, her mind's anchors settle back into place. She is still scared - that last contraction was intense and painful, and she knows that it will get far worse before it gets better – but her man is with her. God sent her to him, and she will try to trust him, and to trust God, and she will try to ignore the sobbing now coming from the stage, try not to think about the man and the bomb and the blade.

She will try not to think about elephants.

Psalms (III)

No-one in the church is looking at the clock as it crosses midday, signalling the end of the morning. A little less than three hours have expired since this strange service began. Time continues to pass.

Chris is transfixed by the sobbing figure on the stage. He stares at the crumpled form. Observes the lowered head and the shaking shoulders, the fist holding all their lives in the balance resting in the lap of this sobbing man. He feels his hollow insides fill up with dread. They're not going to make it. He's not going to make it. He's going to crack, the strain will get to him, or the despair, and all it will take is a second of inattention or failure, shit, even just a tremble, a spasm of some kind, and that's all she wrote, see ya later alligator, they're all just a collection of limbs floating skyward, blood and fire. Chris keeps seeing the fireball, erupting from the stage, rolling over and through all, consuming. He keeps seeing it, even as he lowers his head and tries to pray. Praying not to any God that might be there, not anymore, but to the figure on the stage; the fragile human form that has the power of destruction held under thumb pressure and is currently sobbing his guts out on the wooden stage.

Please. Please don't kill us all.

His prayer matches Katie's word for word. She too has

abandoned attempts to reach outside the walls of the building. Without even realising it, she has started praying to the bomber, attempting to beam thoughts and feelings directly into his brain, hoping somehow to sway him, move him off this path. *Please don't kill us all. Please have mercy on us. Please let us live.* She is becoming aware of a pressing need to pee, is becoming afraid that if this isn't resolved soon, she will wee in her pants, the first time she will have done such a thing since infant school. A thing that before this day began she would have described as impossible, unthinkable.

But here she is. And the pressure is building, and so is the fear, and neither shows any sign of abating. She's going to pee herself. She's going to die in this place. She's going to die with knickers full of wee, and somehow it is this last that is so... upsetting. It's the humiliation; that's all, the feeling of being reduced back to animal function. Horrible. She sends prayers to the huddled figure on the stage, her fear and need to pee growing in tandem, and behind both, a feeling she does not yet recognise as hatred begins to unfurl in her gut.

Deborah has lost all sense of time. Eyes shut; she sees herself floating in darkness, seated on a throne of nothing, up and down existing only as concepts in her mind. She floats. She focuses. Her anger now feels like a physical force as it rolls through her body, like a viscous fluid. She sends it up into her mind, feels her synapses firing and re-wiring in some exciting new configuration, sends it shooting down her arms, the wave giving her muscles strength, vitality. She returns it to her gut and feels her stomach muscles, well- defined thanks to the chair, contract, creating a wall. She imagines blades shattering against that wall, unable to pierce her flesh.

She sends it rolling down into her legs now, expecting to feel nothing, feeling nothing, hoping, visualising, and then there is something. A tingle, an itch. Damnably faint but undeniably there. She feels movement, as though the hairs of her legs were standing on end. Just a hint, a ghost of a whisper of a feeling, but it's something, something she's not felt in seven years.

Something real.

She sends more rage down there, filling her legs with a hot, glowing golden energy, burning them out from the inside, willing them to return to her. She bears down with her out breath, pushing down with her body as well as her mind, unaware of the grimace on her face, the fact that she's sweating, that her head is trembling with the effort, she grits her teeth in her bruised jaw and wills the rage deep, to connect...

A sudden jerk causes her eyes to snap open in surprise. She looks first left, then right, face still snarling. The pregnant woman on her left is lying on the ground, eyes shut, sweaty and pale. Her husband holds her hand and looks down at her, his face serene and distant – to Deborah, he looks like an idiot. To her right, the CP boy is twitching, but is looking at his carer, who is wiping drool from his chin. She takes a moment to feed her hate with a fresh wave of contempt for their sheep-like devotion to each other – *they probably really think they can pray their way out of this* – before her eyes travel downward, at which point her breath catches in her throat. She stares and stares, unable to process, blood pounding in her head, heart thumping under her ribs, sweat dripping unnoticed from the point of her nose onto her lap.

Her left foot has moved.

Several seconds pass before she notices she is feeling faint, and there's still a couple more before she realises why and exhales before drawing in a sudden, shivery breath.

Her left foot has moved. It's no longer resting in the cup where it sits; the heel is no longer flush against the back wedge. It's shifted a good couple of inches forward.

She remembers the jerk that took her out of... whatever it was she was doing, and the enormity of what has happened, of what is happening, explodes across her mind, a euphoric rush.

Holy fucking shit.

I have to go back she realises at once, the intuition she's been riding to this point driving harder than ever, and she tries, but at first she can't. Her mind keeps returning to her left foot, so beautifully, impossibly displaced, and she feels like grinning, and that stops her from being angry.

Anger is the key that turned the lock, child. She can't get back there, which is frustrating, and that helps, frustration is a start, she cues into that, imagines dying here with her left foot that same useless couple of inches out of place, and that sparks into anger. She looks up to the stage, at the bomber who is now sobbing, trembling (*how long has he been there? Why is he crying?*), who has brought her so far but will take her no further, may in fact end it all before it's even began, and slowly but surely the anger becomes rage. The hatred returns to her, like a glass of cold water to the desert survivor, and at 12:47, three minutes after her left leg moved under its own volition for the first time in seven years, Deborah closes her eyes and slips back into the darkness to float once more.

Alex is feeling impatient on a level she would not have credited could exist prior to this day. Her demeanour has remained calm, which is some kind of fucking miracle right there, but she feels like her insides have reached a level of vibration that will soon hit the resonating frequency of her own skull, at which point it's going to be Scanners time all over the row in front. She stares at the backs of their heads – an elderly gentleman in a green coat and a hat, an older woman with grey curly hair, some shorthaired 30 something male – imagines them drenched with the blood and grey matter from her exploding head. It should make her feel like smiling, but not today.

She can't shake the feeling that she missed her shot. That's basically the thing. He was right there, and pretty distracted, but the blade and the blood had her nervous. Then her point man backed out on her, and she nearly went anyway, but in the end she couldn't, and now she seethes and tries not to be afraid. It was a good shot, and she doubts like hell she's going to get a better one. Especially now the blade is out. That thing doesn't look like it's just for sticking, she's sure it could slice and dice pretty good if needed, and that is bad news for anyone planning a palace coup.

And she is still planning it. Visualising it, most seconds. Trying to judge the distance to the stage and how quickly she can cover it. Trying to figure out if anyone will get in her way. Most of all, trying to judge if her point man has relocated his testicles. Because whatever shitty odds she's looking at, she knows that they go from anorexic to fucking dysenteric if Mr Sax Player chooses to sit the party out. So she's trying to will him to open his eyes, and he's cheerfully and blissfully ignoring her, face relaxed, almost smiling. The fucker. Like he's in on some really excellent joke, or the good weed. She promises herself that she's going to slap that smug face at least once, just to see what'll happen.

If they make it out.

So she tries to ignore her full and straining bladder, the smells of fear from the bodies of the worshippers turned cattle around her, tries to tune out the whispering voices of doubt in her own mind. Tries to ignore the apparent emotional instability of the dickhead (*what a shocker there, right?*) and the uncomfortable implications that fragility exposes for the rest of them. Evaluating his slumped form, she tries to think only of physical vulnerabilities, lines of attack, the size and shape of his left hand and wrist, the area she will need to isolate and control with all the speed she can muster. She tries to ignore the wretched sobbing that even now continues to shake his frame.

Open your fucking eyes, Saxman. It's time to get this show rolling.

But Mike has no intention at all of opening his eyes. Not yet. God has asked Mike to wait, so Mike waits. God has asked Mike to listen, so Mike listens. He feels the calming light of God's love within him, filling him with light. He doesn't understand why God saw fit to call the preacher to him so soon, but he questions it no more than you would question whether one and one make two. His plan is manifest, that's all Mike knows and all he needs to know, and Mike does as he is instructed. He waits, and he listens.

Mainly what he hears is crying from the stage. The boy. He sobs and snuffles. From the front row, he hears the occasional low moan from the woman who has gone into labour. There's the odd shuffle, sniffle, even a cough or two from the congregation - because it seems that even the threat of imminent annihilation is not enough to prevent *some* people from coughing in church. Minutes pass, the sounds continue, static on the radio, the murmuring before the orchestra seats, noise without signal. Mike listens.

The sounds of crying from the stage dry up eventually. He hears shuffling and a ripple of reaction from the crowd. The boy has regained his feet, apparently. Good. A throat is cleared, loudly. Mike can hear the snot rattling in the boy's throat.

"Has anyone heard from Him?" Mike hears the click in the boy's throat as he swallows.

Mike prepares to open his mouth, his eyes, but

No Mike. Not yet. Wait. Listen.

Again he hears the collective shuffle and movement of the congregation. The fear is like a stifling blanket, choking out life and hope, trapping in suffocating heat. Mike can smell the terror of the congregation, it seems to roll towards him as they move, shrinking away from the boy and his blade and his question. They remember the preacher, thinks Mike, and the warning against false witness – even if any of them had thought they'd heard something, they're not going to say anything now.

"Anyone?"

There's an awful pleading tone in the boy's voice. A desperate longing, thinks Mike.

"Seriously? A church full of people praying for three hours, and no one of you has had a reply? *Nothing?*" The last comes out in a roar, rage and fear blended with blood.

There's a long silence. Mike waits. Mike listens. He listens to the boy's breathing become ragged, start to hitch again. He realises the boy is crying again.

"Look! *Look!* This woman is in labour. She's giving birth to her child right here, a woman of faith, her loving husband in attendance, and I stand here with this fucking bomb ready to rip her and her child and all of the rest of you to bloody chunks..." - there's a few shrieks and yells from the congregation at this last, and Mike feels them flinching back - "...and no-one's heard *anything?*"

There's a thump that causes a few more frightened yells. Mike hears sobbing from somewhere in the pews and gets the first sense of something deeper and earthier along with the smell of sweat. For a moment, he's transported to a urinal in London and the sound of a flick-knife opening behind him...

"Why are you fucking doing this?"

The boy's yelling is louder, as though he had turned in Mike's direction.

"You think I won't do it, is that it? You sadistic fuck, you think you can put her in the way, and I'll just do the right thing? Is that the measure of you? That you cower behind pregnant women and let them take all your shit? The Great and All-Powerful... You really think that I'm going to fall for that? You can see into my heart! Take a good look! I mean it! You're mistaking regret for weakness, and that means you're nowhere near as good as you need to be, because I WILL DO THIS! I sent you the preacher, and I WILL send the rest of these people in pieces, do YOU FUCKING HEAR ME? I WILL DO THIS! So what have you got to say? To them, to me? To this woman and her husband and this innocent child? Anything? Nothing? DO YOU HEAR ME?!?!"

The last feels like it hangs over everything, not echoing exactly, but like it has a weight, a density, that causes it to continue to have presence long after the air molecules have stopped vibrating with the physical passing of the sound itself.

It's time, Mike. Will you be my vessel?

Always, Lord. Always.

Mike opens his eyes.

"I hear you."

Zechariah

The words ring out rich and deep – deeper than Mike's usual speaking voice. At the same time, his eyes open and take in the boy. He's on his knees; head thrown up to the ceiling. Tears cutting tracks across his cheeks and down his neck, blade in one fist and switch in the other.

His head snaps around at the sound of Mike's voice, and their eyes lock. The boy's are watery, bloodshot, but piercing, intense.

There's a long silence. The boy breathes deep; nostrils flaring, almost panting. He's in a state of animal rage, fury driven to the point of distraction, hanging on to the ragged edge of what passes for his reason. Mike's face remains still, hands resting on his sax, eyes not blinking.

It's clearly for the boy to speak. He seems to know it, too. Much of what has happened appears to have been planned for, rehearsed, but it's clear that this moment had not been part of the calculation. Mike remains silent and unmoving.

Eventually. The boy does. "What did you say?"

"I said, I hear you."

The boy nods, taking it in. His eyes flick from side to side, unfocussed, mind trying to process. "You... I'm..." He shakes his head, as if to clear it. Droplets of sweat fly from his damp fringe, leaving a pattern of dark circles on the wooden stage. "You hear me?"

"I hear you."

The boy laughs now, a single bark, a violent exhalation of breath. "What are you saying?"

"I'm saying I hear you."

The boy leaps to his feet, staggers backwards, almost falls, recovers, regains Mike's face with his eyes. His voice drops, just above a whisper, and there's still anger but also a tremble of something else. "You... is that you?"

"What do you think? What do you feel?"

"I..." The hand with the switch comes up to his brow, presses into the flesh there, rubbing hard, eyes screwed shut. "No, you fucking don't. No. No. It's not about what I feel; it's..."

"What do you feel?"

The boy covers the ground to Mike in three steps, bringing them close enough to kiss. The blade comes up as he walks, coming to rest against Mike's throat. The cold steel causes the hairs on Mike's neck to stand up. "I don't know what this is, but you need to remember what I did to the preacher, friend, you need to..."

"Shall I tell them all your name?"

The boy flinches, visibly recoils, and the blade leaves the surface of Mike's skin for a second. Then he lurches forward again, nose just shy of touching Mike's, hot breath coating his face. "That's a fucking bluff! You're just trying to fuck with me; that's..."

"How about your mother's name? Your father's? How about..."

"Fuck you! You're not Him; you're just some fucking second rate sax player that's about to get..."

Mike's voice deepens further, gains volume. To the boy, it seems to gain a booming echo that rolls out across the building. "Do you doubt that the power of God could fill this room right now and bring you to your knees?"

Mike's face, his eyes, do not change – yet somehow they do. Somehow, to the boy, he appears taller, somehow those same placid eyes now appear to have a power and a light and a purpose. The boy blinks rapidly, colour rising in his face, flushing the shade of brick, and he takes a hesitant step back, a second, a third. Still facing Mike, back to the congregation, one more step will send him tumbling over the edge of the stage, but he does not take that step. Instead, he drops his head, mumbles something.

"What?"

The boy lifts his head, and there's something defiant about the way he does it, about the way he holds himself, as he says "No. I don't."

"So then."

"So."

The silence lasts a long time. Then Mike speaks, and it's with his own voice. "May I tell my story?"

The boy seems to relax at this – his shoulders slump a little, and his jaw lowers, no longer clenching in unconscious tension. "Has He gone?"

Mike smiles, hoping the smile does not betray his fear. This young man means to kill them all, he is quite certain, and many, probably most, are not yet ready to die. God is merciful, yes. But this is now Mike's show, not God's.

I am always with you, Mike. Never doubt it.

"He is always with us, he..."

The boy exhales in amusement, and Mike observes he's smiling. He waves his blade hand dismissively. "Yeah, yeah. But I'm not talking to Him now, am I?"

"He hears all. But no, I'm no longer his vessel."

The boy nods several times, the smile fading from his face, eyes narrowed, considering. Mike takes this in and wonders if God will take control again, or if this is going to be the hour that Mike is called to the kingdom. Mike waits. Mike listens.

"You didn't flinch. When I put the blade to you, you didn't flinch. Why not?"

Mike's made a deep and unbreakable commitment to truth, and this moment doesn't feel like a serious test of that commitment. "Couldn't. Wasn't in control."

The boy's eyes narrow even more, face wrinkling, like

he tasted something bitter. "Vessel, was it?"

Mike nods.

"Sounds more like puppet to me."

"If you say so. Either way, it was my honour."

The boy fully winces at this, like he's been caused physical pain. When he talks, his voice is thicker, less stable. "So where is he now?"

"Everywhere."

"Don't take the piss. You're no longer his meat puppet, right? Why not?"

Mike shrugs. It's all he can do. The boy laughs, an ugly jagged sound. Mike thinks of barbed wire dragged over skin, and his stomach turns over.

"Mysterious fucking ways, huh? Perfect." Head shaking, grin like an open wound. "And I suppose He thinks that's it, right? I've spoken with Him, now it's time to let everybody go, is that it? IS THAT WHAT YOU FUCKING THINK?"

"Well, didn't you?"

The question stops the boy cold. His eyes, which have been darting about like they were chasing the deranged path of a flying insect, snap back to Mike's face, seek out and devour. Mike sees so much blackness there, but he does not look away, and he does not flinch. "Do you doubt that your life is on the line here?"

"I do not. I give it willingly, should that be His will."

Mike feels the impasse, allows it to spin out.

"What about my will? What about that?"

"Your will is free – His gift, to do with as you will."

"Does that make any sense to you?"

Another shrug. "He spoke through me. You heard it. He has fulfilled what you asked."

"Like FUCK! He..."

"You felt it, you..."

"...what the FUCK does that prove?!?"

"You felt it. You felt Him."

"Felt? Fucking FELT?!? Shall I tell you something

about feelings, SHALL I?" The boy is yelling now; face contorted with anger, spit spraying from his mouth, unheeded. Panting like a dog. *Barking like a scared dog, too*, thinks Mike, but he says nothing. If the boy wants to talk, he will. Bad idea to try and push. Dangerous, Mike thinks.

Mike waits. Mike listens.

Little by little, breath by breath, the boy brings himself under control. The dam does not burst. He swallows several times before attempting to speak again, and when he does, his voice is smoother – closer to that performer tone he first took to the stage with. "It's not enough to feel. It's never enough. If you take nothing else from this room, I beg you, please take that. It's not enough to feel. It proves nothing."

Pause. The room breathes as one, every eye - apart from Deborah, whose gaze is still turned inward, unaware of what is unfolding - on the back of the boy. The young man, the killer, the bomber, the shithead, the lunatic, the man with the sword and the bomb.

"I need to know. I need to *know*. He knows that. He understands perfectly. He can make that happen..." here he slams the point of his blade to the stage. The resulting bang is not loud, but it elicits some cries from the congregation just the same "...like that. This..." waving the blade at Mike. "...This puppet show achieves nothing. He knows that too. If you're happy to be his puppet, that's fine. But you need to understand that He's leaving you twisting with this shit, because it isn't enough. And He knows it."

Mike nods, believing. Nevertheless... "I understand what you're saying. I do. I'd still like to tell my story. With your permission."

"Why?"

Mike sighs. But he has no choice. "Because I feel that He wants me to."

The boy throws his arms up in exasperation, sending another wave of fear through the congregation. "What did

I just say, man?"

"I know."

"And fucking yet."

"Yeah."

The boy nods again, then shakes his head, feigning sadness, Mike thinks. Perhaps to hide the real thing.

A sigh. "May I have your name?"

"Mike. My name is Mike."

"And do you wish to talk to the congregation, Mike? Do you have testimony? Do you wish to witness us?"

"I do. I wish to give witness to all who can hear me." Never taking his eyes off the boy's. Because, yes, witness to all who can hear, surely. But there's only one person he's actually talking to here. Only one person he wants - needs - to reach.

The boy nods like he understands. Perhaps he does.

"Okay Mike, it's your own time you're wasting. You have the floor." He gestures this last, inviting Mike to step forward. Mike walks slowly to the edge of the stage, looking out for the first time into the faces of all the scared people. Feeling their collective fear. Their collective desire to survive, to live, to not die. He sees and hears and feels and he walks to the edge of the stage and then turns back to the boy, who has also turned to face him.

They stand on the edge of the stage, facing each other, five paces apart, like duellists in Renaissance England, missing only the flintlocks and ridiculous wigs. The boy nods, once, like a bow. Mike takes him in, drawing breath to speak, offering a prayer in his mind as he does: *Lord, be my protector. Lord, be my guide. Lord, give me the words. Lord, I open my mouth, and you speak. Lord, guide my tongue.*

Mike has witnessed before, many times, in churches, on doorsteps, in living rooms and pubs and on the street. He knows the story well, it's always the same and it's always different, and as that breath comes in and the prayer goes up, Mike slips into that place, the place where the story will come and move mountains. *In Jesus' name.*

KIT POWER

At six minutes past one, on the afternoon of the twenty- third of July, in the year of our lord nineteen ninety-five, Mike speaks.

Chronicles (I)

J was a good child, mostly. I didn't shout a lot; I wasn't angry very much or very often. My parents were not religious, but I went to a Church of England school, and we sang hymns and said prayers in assembly. I believed in God. Because the teachers told me so. Because it made sense, that the world was made. That our creator was good, and loved us, and wanted us to be happy. Gave us rules to follow that would keep us all happy. I never prayed at home. My parents, as far as I know, never prayed at home either. But I prayed at school, and I thought they prayed at work."

Mike shrugs.

"It had a logic to it, I suppose. It didn't even occur to me that they... Well, that anyone wouldn't believe. Made no sense to me."

Pause. Looking in the boy's eyes.

"To be honest, it still doesn't."

Nothing.

"Anyway. I was basically a good kid. Popular. Good at sport. Not that great in class. Didn't much care for learning. Just wanted to hang out with my mates, really. Pretty normal.

"My father died when I was twelve. Cancer. He smoked; mum smoked. He got sick quick, diagnosed late. Told me he had it, and three months later he was gone.

"My dad, he was a big man, you know? Strong man.

Plumber by trade, good with his hands. Cancer ate him from the inside. Ate the muscle right off his bones.

"I remember visiting him in hospital, the day... the day he passed. He was dosed to the eyeballs, didn't know we were there. I remember how thin he looked. You could see his skull through the skin of his face. You could... when I held his hand, I remember how his skin felt so dry. Like paper or something.

"He passed on a Sunday. I woke up hearing my mum crying in the kitchen. She'd got the call and just fallen down in the kitchen, sobbing. When I went down there, I saw her sitting on the floor. I knew. I went and sat in her lap, and we cried together. I remember that she held me, but she couldn't stop crying. I remember that her breath was bitter, bad. I remember it made me feel ill - her bitter breath in my face as she cried.

"She never really stopped crying, I don't think. Never stopped mourning him. She started drinking that day. Gin and tonics, as soon as she could stand again. Stayed drunk to the funeral. I remember when everyone else had left, it was just us standing at the grave. She was still crying. I wanted her to stop, to feel better. Wanted it more than I wanted him back, even. I knew he wasn't coming back. So I said 'Mummy, he's in heaven now'."

Mike takes a breath here. None of this is easy, no matter how many times he tells it – but this part is the worst for him. He can't tell it without feeling it again. The shame. The hurt.

"She... She went very still. Then she squatted, so we were face to face. She looked me in the eyes. Then she hit me."

Mike swallows, somehow does not choke.

"It was a proper wallop – my mum could pack a good one when she needed to. It hurt. I cried out in pain, I remember that. Then she grabbed my shoulders, squeezing really hard. 'Don't you ever talk that crap to me again. Don't! You! Ever!' each time..."

Mike mimes shaking a child.

"... like this. She was so cross; she got spit on my face. I said sorry, and then she sat back and really started wailing. I tried to hug her, but she was just limp. I held on anyway.

"She never hit me again. She just withdrew. From me, from everything. She stopped working. Kept drinking. Kept smoking too. I'd come home from school, see her sitting there on the sofa, watching soaps, smoke in one hand and G and T in the other. If I close my eyes..."

He does so.

"...I can still see her like that."

He opens his eyes again, his gaze settling on the face of the boy, but his sight has turned inward.

"I stopped praying. In assembly, whenever we were supposed to bow our heads, I'd just stare at the teachers who were supposed to make sure we were doing it. They knew I'd lost my dad. They left me alone.

"And I started smoking. Getting the fags was easy. Mum bought them by the box, so I'd just rob packs out of there whenever I wanted. I'd hear her swearing about it sometimes, muttering about how fast she was getting through them. Complaining about the price.

"And I started drinking. Again, it was easy. She stopped getting up in the mornings, you see. Was always sleeping off the night before. I'd just take gin from the bottle she'd been on the previous evening. Put it in a juice bottle. Hide it under my bed. The smell made me feel sick, so I'd mix it up with lemonade to try and make it taste better.

"The first time I did it, I had no idea about how much I should drink. How much was too much. I got really sick. I remember hugging the bowl of the toilet, really heaving my guts out. That really bitter taste you get when you can't puke anymore, but you can't stop. I could hear the sound of the TV coming through the floor. It sounded like a nightmare, all muffled and distorted. Horrible. Could smell the cigarette smoke too. I remember thinking 'God, I want to die. Just let me die, God.' I woke up in the early hours, asleep on the toilet floor. Had a towel for a blanket. Probably I just pulled it over myself. But I remember thinking that maybe Mum had done it. Seen me asleep on the floor and covered me."

Mike blinks rapidly, sending a single tear running down his cheek. He appears not to notice this.

"Started getting in fights too, at school. Kids... kids smell weakness. Doesn't matter how popular you are. If you look weak, act weak... Well, you know. They knew how to hurt me, and they did. Being a big kid, I hurt 'em back. They'd say something about my dad, and I'd throw a fist. The first kid, I beat him so badly he had to be sent home, didn't come back for a week. The teachers knew what the boy had said, so I didn't get in big trouble, but they made it clear that I couldn't keep lashing out.

"But the taunts kept coming, and I couldn't stop myself. And after a couple more fights, I started getting detentions. On the last day of term, during the afternoon break, it was one of the girls who started mouthing off. Saying she'd heard my dad died of syphilis, from being gay."

Pause.

"People talk about the red mist, right? They say when you get that angry, you lose control. Stop thinking. It wasn't like that for me. I knew exactly what I was doing. I looked around, saw Kenny with his cricket bat. I took it off him, pulled it out of his hands, pushed him over. He fell on his bum as I turned around. I didn't feel anything. I walked up to the girl. She had that 'what are you looking at' face. And one of those angry smiles. Like when someone is glad they hurt you.

"She was still smiling like that when the bat hit her jaw. I think she thought I was just threatening her; that I was going to pull it at the last minute. She didn't want to show she was scared. Didn't want to lose face."

Mike can't help but laugh, even though he feels sick with shame.

"Her lower jaw went sideways. I remember feeling the impact all the way up my arm as the end of the bat hit her face. It just went sideways. There was a crack, louder than the smack of the wood. I saw..."

He swallows, does not retch.

"...I saw a tooth come out her mouth. Blood and spit. I remember staring in her eyes. I remember her face frozen, total shock. I could hear footsteps across the gravel; someone running and yelling. But I couldn't take my eyes off her face. I looked her in the eyes. Saw the tears welling, the total shock. And I smiled.

"Then the teacher rugby tackled me hard enough that I was knocked out when my head hit the ground.

"I was lucky on that score, at least. The concussion put me in hospital, so I didn't end up going straight to the police station. I was out of it for a while. When I came around, my mum was in the room. She looked terrible. Really old. Like she'd been crying a lot, you know? Yeah. She said I was a disappointment, a disgrace. Said she didn't want anything more to do with me. Said I disgusted her. She said..."

As often happens at this part, Mike hesitates, and in his mind hears his father's voice: *'Tell it, son. Tell the truth and shame the devil'.*

He swallows.

"She said my dad would be ashamed of me. Then she left me in the hospital. I think... I think she stuck around just to make sure I wasn't going to die. Once she knew that, she didn't care anymore.

"I knew I had to run away. I mean, they were going to arrest me, put me in a borstal for all I knew. And even if they didn't, I couldn't go back to that school, or to that house. I didn't have it in me. I was meant to be staying in one last night for observation, so I waited until the evening shift change, and I just snuck off.

"Getting home was scary – I knew the route, but it was too far to walk, so I hitched. I got lucky, made it back to the house okay. I used the spare key, under the plant pot. She was already passed out on the couch. I took a couple of changes of clothes, the carton of fags, two bottles of gin and all the cash in her purse, about forty quid. Never left a note. Just took what I needed and left."

Mike pauses, lost in the flow of memory, the pulls of the currents. He remembers so much when he talks like this, recalls things long past, buried. It's not him, he knows, it's God's work, no question. He feels the power of the story. How much to tell? What matters?

Let go and let God.

"The cash got me to London. I knew that was where I wanted to go. I remember getting off the train, the crush of people. Totally overwhelming. I remember feeling scared then. Really scared. And... trapped. I had nowhere to go back to, and nowhere to go to either. It was horrible. I felt lost. I was lost. I thought about throwing myself under one of the trains. But I couldn't. I was too scared of how much it would hurt."

Pause.

"That was the first time I can remember thinking about killing myself. Thirteen years old at Euston train station.

"Anyway. I didn't die. Got good at begging, instead. There were a lot of homeless around the station. Lots of drunks, junkies. They took me in, basically. It helped that I had gin to share. And after a few days under the arches, I looked pitiful enough that people'd give me change.

"That became my life, very quickly. Beg for money, money for booze and food, crash under the arches. It actually wasn't so bad. No-one made fun of me or tried to make me angry. Nobody knew me. I remember people tried to rob me a couple of times, but I was strong enough to fight them off. I looked hard enough that most didn't bother anyway.

"Gradually, I found out about shelters, places I could get a free meal, a bed for the night. That gave me more money to spend on booze. And somewhere along the way...

"No, I suppose I need to tell it, don't I? There was a girl. Billy. She begged outside Kings Cross a lot. And she turned tricks too, when the money was tight. She took a bit of a shine to me. She was older. I don't know how old – never did find out. She liked me. I think mainly because I was big. She thought I could protect her. Anyway. We became friends. Lovers. And she had been using heroin since she was twelve, so when she told me how it felt, how it made all the bad things go away..."

It's like he's back at the NA meeting when he finally decided to share, the story pouring out of him like a flood. Not how he normally tells it with a church audience, but it feels right. In fact, it feels good. There's a cleansing to it, laying bare all the scars for inspection. It all serves to make the Glory that much greater.

"I wasn't hard to convince. And I liked her too. Didn't want to seem like a wimp. So I did it with her. And it was like... It was like falling in love. Really. All the love songs I'd heard suddenly made sense. This was the feeling. This stuff was love. It was pure. It took away all the pain, just like she said. It all went away.

"Somewhere around here, we found ourselves a squat, so we had a base. It was cold in the winter, but it was year round dry, somewhere we could huddle up. Keep each other warm.

"The heroin was better than the booze, but I'd been drunk every day since I ran away, and I'd been on the street by now almost a year. So I needed both. And of course, with smack, there's really no such thing as enough.

"So I begged, and occasionally shoplifted, and Billy went back to turning tricks."

It's like having a bad road accident on a bike; he thinks. *You end up with lumps of gravel under the skin.*

"I could tell you I tried to argue, or stop her. But I didn't. The truth is I didn't much care what she did, as long as she brought back the smack and as long as she shared. And she did. She always did. She got beaten up pretty badly a couple of times, I remember that. One time, I remember waking up next to her, it was the middle of the night I think, and seeing blood soaking into her pants, like she'd been cut. I rolled over and went back to sleep. When I woke up, the blood was gone.

"Time works different when you're high all the time. There's basically two types of time: gear time, and no gear time. Gear time is good, obviously, but it really flies by. If you've got a good supply, gear time can eat up days and weeks. Easy. When you're out of gear and cash, though, when it's been a few hours and you've got no money and you don't know how you're going to get some, that's when every minute crawls by. Time slows down and down until you think you're going to die, because of how long each breath takes. And you sort of don't mind dying, really, except you think you'd miss getting high again, and that was always enough to keep me going.

"We got moved on, of course. London's always bulldozing and rebuilding. We managed to stay one step ahead of the bailiffs, find a new spot. And most of the time was gear time, and the months and seasons just fell away from me. I got to where I couldn't tell you what day of the week, what month it was. I had a sense of the seasons thanks to the weather, but that's as far as I could do with the passing of time. We stayed high; we stayed together, I begged and stole; she begged and turned tricks.

"You've always got something to do; that's the thing. Either getting to where you can score or getting high."

Mike smiles.

"Busy, busy, busy.

"Billy died in the winter of nineteen seventy nine. She'd gotten painfully thin by that point, and the tricks had turned cheaper and meaner. One of them broke her nose, and it didn't set right, and that made working harder. It made her better for begging, but it was less reliable money, and we'd gotten used to how much she could bring in tricking. Gotten used to the amount of smack we could get through in a week. So when our earnings went down, it was bad. We both got sick that winter. Looking back, I couldn't tell you where illness took off and withdrawal began.

"Anyway. We got sick, which got us out less, which made the begging harder. Less money, less smack. Vicious circle. And then the snow came. We'd been through a cold one the year before, but this was something else. It just fell and fell and fell. The city pretty much ground to a halt. No-one going anywhere. I remember when we woke up and saw it, two feet deep and still falling, Billy just looked at it and back at me and burst into tears.

"We cooked up everything we had left, loaded two spikes, and then cuddled up together, all our clothes on; blankets wrapped around us. We just huddled together in the corner and nodded off. I remember feeling her tremble under all the layers. I remember how I could see my breath, pulling a blanket up over my face. I remember nodding out. I remember thinking 'I don't care if I don't wake up'."

Mike is lost now, completely swept away by the wave of memory. Mouth moving on automatic, mind turning pictures and feelings into words as best it can.

"I did wake up, eventually. It was still cold. Bitter. The first thing I remember was I couldn't feel the end of my nose. She was wrapped around me, like another layer of bedding. Not moving. We both had all our clothes on. I remember holding her tighter, trying to feel a breath. But her face was on my shoulder, and I couldn't see her breath, couldn't feel it on my skin.

"She was still warm, on the side pressed against me. But I knew... I knew.

"Couldn't tell you how long I sat there. Couldn't tell you. I tried to pretend it was a dream; then I tried pretending it was a game, that she was just holding her breath.

"Then I tried pretending I was dead too. Held my breath a few times, feeling the world go grey, but I always came back. I wasn't dead. She was.

"Eventually, I managed to get up. She was dead weight, but so thin. It wasn't hard to untangle myself. Standing was tougher, I remember that. Not sure how many days we'd been there, but my legs didn't want to get under me. Eventually, they did. I just stood, leaning against the wall. I looked down and saw her, still hugging my legs, face resting on my boot."

Did he need to tell them that he saw her still, when he closed his eyes, in his dreams? He thinks not. He thinks they know. He thinks maybe they see her too, now.

"Eventually I left the squat. Never went back. Didn't tell anyone. What could I say? I felt hollowed out, by the cold and the junk. Like there was nothing inside of me. Walked through the snow. Eventually found a church, lights on. I was cold to the bone by then, shivering really hard, teeth proper rattling in my head. I didn't have a plan, but when I saw the light, I was just pulled in.

"The church was busy, despite the snow. Maybe because, I don't know. I sat at the back. There were heaters in the aisle, and I sat near one, ignoring the service and the hymns and all that, just letting the heat into me, trying to suck it up as best I could. By the time the service was over, I felt halfway alive again. It felt like what I'd just been through was melting along with my skin unfreezing.

"At the end, people lined up to get out, shaking hands with the vicar. I stayed back, hanging around the heat and hoping I could avoid having to do that, but he stuck around, and it was pretty clear I wasn't going to get away. So I shuffled past and shook his hand when he offered it. His grip was strong, and I looked up into his eyes. They seemed kind. I mumbled thank you, feeling ashamed. He asked if I was on the street. I said I was. He was still holding my hand, and I remember worrying he was going to start preaching at me or something, but instead he took a fiver out of the collection plate and gave it to me. 'Go with God,' he said with a smile. I thanked him again. Even managed a smile. A real one."

Mike's eyes lock onto the boy's, snapping back into focus from the long past to the bleeding present.

"Because now I knew I'd be able to score."

Mike smiles, the same tight smile he had on that day, and he sees the boy's face crinkle around the eyes, sees he is grinning back. He holds the moment, the smile, and the boy laughs, and as he does, so he lowers his head, shaking it, still chuckling. Mike's gaze follows him down, then snaps into the congregation, stage left three rows down, aisle seat, and he locks onto the blazing eyes of the young woman with the short hair. His friend. He raises an eyebrow, just a fraction. Her face explodes with a grin that vanishes almost as soon as it's appeared, warming his whole body. She inclines her head, raising her brow, and Mike allows his left hand to twitch down once, at his side.

Not now. Soon. Be ready.

She looks to Mike like she was born ready.

The boy's head is raising, and Mike snaps his focus back, suddenly scared he's given himself away, but the boy is slow, and the dancing in his eyes suggests he's still amused, enjoying the punch line.

"May I tell the rest? There's plenty more to tell."

"Of course, Mike. We've got nothing better to do. The stage is yours."

I hope you're right about that, thinks Mike.

Chronicles (II)

Mike turns his attention back to the boy, refocuses his mind. Tell the story, yes. Tell it true. Tell it true enough to draw all of him in and hold him. *With your help, Lord. In your name.*

"So, I went and scored. Then found a shelter. They were pretty much open door at that point, filled to busting because of the weather. So they let in anyone that turned up, and we were sleeping everywhere. On the floor, in the kitchens and offices. I was underneath one of the bunk beds. The woman who was in the mattress above me had really terrible wind. Kept me awake all night with her farts."

Another chuckle, answered by the boy.

"Honestly! It was grim, man. She let rip a good one every ten minutes or so, and I'd just start to drift back off from the noise when the smell hit." Mike pulls a face. "Foul, man. Absolutely foul. Anyway, the snow lasted a week, and then things started getting back to normal. It was still cold out, but I had the shelters of an evening – they were easier to get into single than they had been when it was me and Billy – and I begged and blagged during the day. The only difficult part was hiding the shooting up from the others in the shelter. Didn't want to get thrown out. Really didn't want to have to share.

"I needed the junk, though. I mean, it'd had hold of my body for a while, but now it really ran my mind too. High was the only time I didn't think about her. And I needed to not think about her, if you get me." He sees something change in the boy's face.

Direct hit. Be careful now. You have him, but... be careful.

"I think maybe I would have lived that life until it killed me. It felt... not right, because it doesn't feel right. But it felt, umm, okay, I guess. I think I thought I deserved it. Maybe I did.

"I managed over a year just like that. I was slowly getting sicker. Didn't care. My youth was drying up, which made the begging tougher. Money got tighter. Smack harder to buy. The shoplifting kept me afloat, but it was getting hairy. I remember one time, running down Oxford Street, I only got away because I jumped over a baby in a pushchair. I heard the security guard run into it. Heard the baby screaming. The woman too. Didn't look back.

"Anyway. Long story slightly less long – I got into dealing. I was big for my age, looked old enough to be a student. My dealer was into everything, and he had an opening in the local Poly's Student Union. I didn't ask why. Just took the job. He cleaned me up a bit, took my picture and gave me a fake student union pass, speed balls, weed bags and some coke, and told me the prices. I got paid in H, the good stuff.

"It was a pretty sweet deal. I knew if I got caught I'd be in trouble, and I knew damn well I'd have to take the fall on my own, but I was young. Figured there was a good chance I'd stay out of prison. And I needed a fix. That's really all it came down to."

Mike takes a single step towards the boy, looking right at him but also looking through him, down the barrel of the evening he is seeking to bring back as whole as he can from the depths of his brain. Willing it to be real.

"That evening was going pretty well. It was Friday night; there was a big crowd in for the bands. Security was non-existent, really. The kids were looking to party. It was a couple of weeks after grant day. There was some touring band headlining. I barely got out of the toilet all night. Making sales, switching cash for little bags. I did all the deals one to one, in a cubicle. Door shut. There'd been a queue, I remember that. I had a wedge of notes, and a lot of coin as well.

"It wasn't till the second band came on that business finally tailed off. I remember zipping the cash in my jacket pockets. Doing a quick stock check. Not much left. Leaving the cubicle, then remembering that I'd been holding in a pee for the last couple of hours. It's funny how you can spend that long in the toilet and forget what it's supposed to be used for.

"So instead of turning left, to the exit, I turned right, walked across the room..."

Mike, lost in the story, takes a step forward, towards the boy. Three paces away now.

"...over to the trough. I was mid flow when I heard the door open. I heard three sets of footsteps. The first two came in and stopped behind me."

Mike takes a step, this time moving diagonally, still towards the boy but also away from the edge of the stage, causing the boy to turn towards him.

Away from the congregation.

The boy has a look on his face Mike recognises well from AA and NA, normally on the faces of the serial relapsers, the ones who fail to connect with a higher power. It's a look of hunger. The look of someone who just loves the smell of a barbecue.

Bring it home, Mike, he thinks to himself.

"One of them about where I am to you. The other..." Mike points across the stage. The boy turns further to see the spot, then looks back to Mike. "... about there.

"The third one stayed by the door. That's how I knew I was in trouble.

"Have you ever tried to stop doing your business before you're finished?" Mike grins, shakes his head. "Well, I'll tell you, you can do it if you have to, but it really hurts. I managed it though, tucked myself away, zipped. I went to turn around, wanted to see what I was dealing with, but the guy here..."

Pointing at his own chest.

"...said 'Don't turn around'. So I didn't. I felt... I can't really describe it. I should have been panicked, but I wasn't. I remember just feeling really aware of everything. The smell of the urine and the soap and the yellow things in the trough. The sound of the band just a dull thudding through the wall. The peeling red paint on the wall above the tiles in front of me. The frosted glass on the thin window. The metal safety bar to open it.

"I heard the cloth of his jacket move as he lifted his arm..." Mike raises his own fist to waist height, pointing forward. "...and I heard the click of a blade."

Mike mimes pressing a button, violently, and the boy looks down, and Mike's eyes flick over his shoulder and meet the eyes of the young woman. Time is moving super slow now, and he has time to see the colour in her cheeks, her elevated breathing. He sees this even in the less than half-second he takes her in, just in a slight shudder as she inhales. He sees the fire in her eyes, has time to be utterly struck by her beauty. She is transcendent. His eyes drag themselves back to the boy in the barest nick of time. The boy realises there was some eye movement but doesn't know what, and Mike holds his gaze and nods, peripheral vision picking up that she has gotten the signal and is on the move, she is rolling, and by God, she's got pace. All Mike has to do is hold this boy for four more seconds. Mike smiles, starts to talk, it all feels to be happening at the speed of pouring treacle, but that's fine, she takes the first step and Mike says

"I knew..."

Her second step, and Mike's talking just a bit too fast, the words almost running into each other, adrenaline making itself known, but it fits the story, and Mike says

"...then that..."

She's two steps away, and close enough that Mike can see her hands are up and to her left, she's going for the switch. She gets it. She understands. Mike realises that she's going to knock the kid right into him, probably, but that's okay as long as she gets the switch, and he's sure she will. Her rubber soled boots hit the ground, blessedly making no noise, and Mike says

"...unless..."

He has time to see the boy's eyes begin to widen in recognition, like he suddenly understands where the story is going...

Genesis

The explosion is deafening in the enclosed space.

Revelation (I)

Alex doesn't understand. She's looking at the switch, all of her concentration on that one spot, the fist and the button everything that she is bent on reaching, taking.

The switch is still being held. The hyper-reality of the moment, time slowed by adrenaline, allows her to see this, to fail to process it. Then she is punched in the back, hard. Immediately, her legs go limp, suddenly refusing to obey her command. She feels herself pitching forwards. She's already arching backwards in reaction to the blow, so she falls sideways, the landing hard enough to knock the wind out of her and really hurt, but she doesn't bang her head, so there's that.

She can hear shouts, screams, a yell from the stage, the sound of something heavy and metal hitting the ground. *Sounds like Mike is going for plan B, good deal.* Then a voice from the back of the hall yells

"STOP!"

The struggling sounds cease. All Alex can see at the moment is the edge of the stage itself and the feet and wheels of the people in the front row, on the other side of the aisle. She notices with the detached clarity of someone on the edge of shock that one of the sets of legs in a wheelchair appear to be shaking, as though the owner were cold or had some kind of palsy. She can picture in her mind Mike and the fuckhead, frozen in some kind of wrestling stance.

What she can't figure out is why.

Also, why her legs have stopped working. They don't appear to be hurting, she realises. In fact, as she thinks about it, they don't seem to be feeling much of anything at all.

She feels the weight of something turning in her mind.

"Mike, you need to let go now!"

Don't you fucking dare, Mike.

"I can't." Mike sounds a little ragged as he replies, but also firm. *Good deal.* Alex makes fists, experimentally. This appears to work. She raises her right arm to her face to verify. *Systems normal, captain. So what the fuck...*

"You have to, Mike." The voice from behind her trembles with tension.

"He'll kill us all." Mike sounds calmer, somehow. Still clear. Alex twists her head away from the stage, looking down the aisle towards the source of the hoarse, scared voice making the demands.

She's ground level, so her first sight is his boots. Doc Martens? Combats? Something like that. One planted in front of the other; the back leg braced. It's a pose she recognises, but can't place, though the sound of the explosion comes roaring back in her memory. She sees the leather coat, ankle length, hanging open, the black jeans beneath, plain belt, an improbable white shirt, ironed and tucked in. His arms are held out in front of him rather than by his side.

That's when she sees the gun.

He's holding it out, pointed down the aisle. It's a handgun, pistol, something. He's holding it in his left hand, right bracing his wrist, and the pose comes back to Alex from a million dumb cop programs on TV as a kid, from TJ Hooker on down.

Even with the double grip, the barrel is trembling, and the brow of the face that she can see behind the sight of the gun looks terrified. Crazy.

Don't shit it, Mike, she thinks. *This motherfucker's too scared to shoot anyone.*

That's when she spots the last wisp of smoke leaving the barrel.

That's when she looks down at her stomach.

She's wearing a purple shirt, and she watches with a rapidly detaching interest as the blood blooms and spreads, soaking into the fabric like a burning fuse, staining the silk dark, racing out in all directions. The explosion, the blow to the back, her legs...

Shot in the back. Bleeding out of her front. Can't feel her legs. *That's probably bad,* she thinks, as the icy waters of shock embrace her like an unforgiving lover and pull her under. Just before conscious thought leaves her, she hears a woman screaming in pain and fear, and the sound follows her into the dark.

It's Emma screaming. The gunshot was too much. The dam her and her husband had been building against the lake of fear is breached. Her body is flooded with chemicals, carrying the frantic message through her bloodstream from her fevered brain – *we are dying, danger, danger, eject, eject. Save the child, bring the child* now.

It's too soon, too much. Her body hasn't done this before, after all. A second or third child, the biology gains a muscle memory. The first time is always the hardest. And the same fear that triggers the new and powerful contraction drives tension into her body in places where it's not helpful, adding resistance to force. The pressure is tremendous, and she feels as though she's being torn apart down there. Like the passing of the child is going to take her guts with it. She's mostly okay with that, but she's afraid that the terror will also act on the child. That it will feel her distress, and added to the trauma of being born, something bad will happen to her baby, and fear piles fear into terror until the pain and drive force everything aside and she becomes what she is: An animal, pushing a life into the world.

"Say again?" Mike can't hear the shooter over the screams of the woman birthing in front of the stage. Also, he wants to buy time. He's waiting on God, wondering if he'll hear that voice again. Because right now, he doesn't know what to do.

"I SAID; HE WON'T DO IT." The shooters face flushes with the effort of yelling.

Mike jerks the fist he has clamped in both his own forward for emphasis. "He can't! Why would I..."

There's a blast of pain in his temple as the boy pounds his head with his free fist. Mike has time to be grateful that he made the boy drop the blade, and then he's hit again, even harder. He staggers a half step back, hands clenched like a vice, dragging the boy with him, causing him to stumble too, and for a nightmarish second Mike thinks they are both going over, that he will slip, his grip will loosen, and it will all end in fire. Then he regains balance, shoves forward. As the boy regains his centre and reaches back for another blow, Mike steps towards him and flings his forehead at the boy's face.

Even through the pain of the impact, Mike feels the boy's nose give way with a very satisfying crunch.

The boy's knees weaken, and they stagger again, but Mike is ready for this and digs his heels in, bracing his arm. He can feel the imprint of the boy's nose on his forehead, can also feel a warmth that may be his blood, but is more likely the boy's. Both hands hold the boy in place as he twists around his trapped hand, and yes, Mike sees, his nose is bleeding pretty heavily already, twin tracks of red running over his lips, joining together to drip from his chin. The boy shrieks in pain, tears popping from his eyes, spare hand going to his damaged face, holding the air in front of his nose. Mike feels a sudden urge, very powerful, to just pummel this kid's head until he's out.

It seems like the best plan.

He starts to pull the kid back to his feet, meaning to move in with the head again, not intending for a moment to relax his hands.

There's a second gunshot, and the glass window high in the wall above their heads shatters.

"ENOUGH, ENOUGH!"

Mike looks up.

Katie feels something in her head let go. The fear has built and built and built, become unbearable. That girl tried to stop the madman while the sax player distracted him, and Katie saw it all, was sure, *convinced* that it was going to work, and she felt the fear melt in her heart, hope instead surging like a warm flood in her chest. *Of course,* the girl is going to save them, *of course,* they're not going to die here, *of course* God won't...

The gunshot was deafening, and Katie was far from being the only person in the congregation whose overstrained bladder took the opportunity to release. She felt the flower wither and die and grow thick, barbed thorns that tore at her insides, becoming a black weed worse than fear. Despair ripped at her as she watched the girl collapse, and for a few precious seconds, as the urine runs down her legs and stains her jeans, she is lost to herself, to everything, consumed by darkness.

Then she hears the second shot, the voice yelling "ENOUGH!", and she realises she agrees one thousand percent with that particular sentiment. Before she can even give herself time to think, she's on the move, because fuck it, she's going to die, probably they all are, stinking in her own piss, but she's damned if she's not going to live first. This thought seems to detonate in her gut, burning away the crippling darkness like it never was, and she moves her unlocked limbs.

She turns, and the bald sweaty man stares at her, and he

is frowning, his eyes are watery, but Katie has decided to move, so her gaze does no more than brush his face as she starts to walk, and so she is surprised when his arm blocks her way.

"Please, don't it's not..."

"I have to; I have..."

"No, please..."

The anger explodes in her, through her, like a lightning strike, and she elbows him in the stomach. She hears his surprised exhalation, and his arm drops and she is not running but striding fast down the pew. The remaining people in her aisle sweep their legs to one side, avoiding eye contact, as she moves into and across the aisle, kneeling by the head of the fallen girl. She's dead pale; her face milk white, almost waxy, and her eyes are staring blankly, no focus, but pupils the same size and she's drawing breath.

"What are you doing?"

It's the shooter. His voice is wobbly. She doesn't look up, taking the legs of the girl, untangling and straightening them out. Trying to make her comfortable.

"I'm helping her. I want to help her. Shoot me or leave me alone."

She says it calm, she feels calm, that same thought – *I'm going to die here, so I might as well live* – holds her tight. Her heart is beating fast and heavy, but she feels okay as she takes off her jacket and puts it under the girl's head.

The second shot forces Deborah to surface. It's an effort. Precious seconds tick as she forces open her eyes, bringing her back into the room, into the light. Her first instinct is to look down, and sure enough, both legs have moved this time – her left foot is now more than halfway off the step it normally rests on, and her right is at a different angle.

Holy shit.

She's actually doing this.

She looks to the stage next, taking in the scene. The sax player has his fists clamped around the trigger switch, the young man's face is bloody, and she has time to wonder what she's missed, when a voice from behind her, wobbling with emotion, says, "Next bullet is aimed at you. Of course, I'm not a great shot. I might miss you and hit him."

It's like a bucket of ice-cold water over her head. Panic drenches Deborah, she feels sweat ripple out of her pores, gut cramping. *Too fucking soon.* Too soon, she's not ready. She tries anyway, tries to move, tries to stand. She feels a tingling, like the numbness before pins and needles kicks in, and she sees her thighs trembling, but whatever it is that's happening to her, it's not happening quickly enough, so instead she yells, "GET BEHIND HIM!"

Chris sees Mike, witnesses the realisation burst, like on the face of a remedial child who successfully makes it to the potty, and Chris hates him with all his heart. For what he's making him do. Offering up a silent prayer of his own, Chris closes one eye and, just as Mike starts to twist behind the bomber, he pulls the trigger again.

The adrenaline to move is still running through Mike's body, not having yet reached his muscles, when the bullet catches him high in the right shoulder, shattering his collarbone and spitting bone fragments from the exit wound. The blow twists Mike away from the boy, and his hand, instantly numb, drops its grip. The boy, damnably quick, spins and punches Mike with all his strength in the fresh wound, and the spike of pain is monstrous, driving Mike to his knees, his other hand moving to cover the bleeding hole instinctively, freeing the boy. Mike has time to take this in, as he kneels; warm blood beginning to flow down his arm, across his chest, under his shirt. He sees the boy's face twist into a savage grin of victory, watches as he takes a step back, plants, and swings his foot forward.

Mike doesn't even try and move, and the boot is still accelerating when it connects with his jaw. His teeth crack together, he sees spots burst into his field of vision, he is aware that he is moving, falling, but the world is suddenly distant, fading. *I am being called to the kingdom*, thinks Mike, *it's my time*, and he has time to think this, time to wonder and regret and not regret, and then the flooring of the stage comes up to meet his still accelerating head, and there's a second smash of pain across the back of his skull, and an interval of blessed oblivion.

Consciousness returns slowly. There's an angry voice, shouting, but Mike cannot make out the words – the sound appears to fade in and out, like an old TV with a dodgy signal. He's aware of pain – in and behind his eyes, his skull, his shoulder, which appears to be burning. He feels the boards he's resting on shifting, like someone is walking about. The sounds still won't make words – or rather, they do, but he hears them without understanding, each word floating into his mind, then pop, gone, leaving behind no impression, no meaning. He feels dizzy, like the bad hangovers, the ones he got a lot towards the end, and he thinks that if he's dying, it's pretty shitty that he should die feeling hungover without even having had a drink, and that's when God speaks to him, one last time.

Mike listens.

Deborah's eyes are glued to the stage as the young man, ranting speech over (she'd particularly enjoyed how his m sounds have all become b sounds, thanks to his remodelled nose), picks up the blade and walks over to Mike. *Don't open your eyes*, she thinks. *If you're out, stay out. You don't want to stick around for this.*

The young man turns the blade point down, above

Mike's stomach, and she wants to yell, to make him stop or at least pause, but she can't find her voice. Doesn't want to be next. So she does not yell, and she does not turn away, and the bomber raises the blade as high as he can before bringing it down hard, actually falling to his knees as he drives the sword into Mike's stomach.

She does not look away as Mike's eyes fly open, bulging, his mouth gaping and working a silent scream. She does not look away as the young man leans on the blade, forcing it deeper, causing Mike's eyes to roll back in his head before snapping back into focus. She does not look away as the young man yells wordlessly, fury and victory and loss and terror, causing her to wonder if this is the moment it ends for all of them.

And so, because she does not look away, she sees Mike's arm come up fast, grabbing the young man's collar, yanking his suddenly scared face down to Mike's. For a glorious moment, Deborah thinks Mike is going to bite his face, perhaps chew his ear off even, and she feels a bitter joy rise in her chest. Instead, she sees Mike's lips moving, breathing laboured, forcing some final message out. Deborah watches the face of the young man as this happens, and is amazed at the journey it takes – the fear fades into some neutral expression, which gradually becomes paler and paler, blood draining from his face, then the corners of his mouth pull down, like an upside down smile, his brow starts to furrow, and Deborah's waning joy surges back as exhilaration. For some reason, she's reminded of the old joke about the crying donkey and the cowboy in a bar – the one where the cowboy makes the donkey laugh by whispering something, then later makes him cry again, and the barman asks how he did it, and the cowboy says 'the first time, I told him I had a bigger dick than him, and the second time, I showed him'. It runs through her mind in an instant, as the storm in the young man's face builds and builds, and the lightning is likely to be terrible and the thunder may just kill them all, but Deborah cares not a bit, she is surging and pulsing with pleasure as Mike drives the words into the young man's mind like needles, like spikes.

Fuck him up, Mike. Fuck him up good. For me. For all of us.

The hand on the blade begins to tremble, and that makes it move inside of Mike, and Mike can no longer talk, breath driven from his body. The young man takes the opportunity to escape Mike's grip and rises to his feet, straining to pull out the blade as he does so. Mike roars in pain, head flung back as the blade leaves him, and Deborah observes a spray of blood flick from the edge of the sabre as the boy raises it above his head, point to the ceiling.

He does not pause at the top of the swing, bringing the blade down again hard, again dropping to his knees as he falls. Deborah does not look away as the blade passes through Mike's throat, sending a spray of bright blood in a fountain that rises over the edge of the stage, splashing the face of the labouring woman on the floor underneath.

Mike's head turns, falls, rolls in the socket, loose and uncontrolled, eyes open, sightless, and those in the congregation who look see only their own fear reflected back at them. His leg is twitching, spasming, but the fountain of blood has already begun to slow, to trickle. *Gone*, thinks Deborah. *Passed*.

She turns her attention back to the young man. The fist that holds the blade is now red, the blood glistening in the sunlight beaming through the shattered window behind him. That same light casts his face in shadow, but Deborah can make out his features well enough. He is still very pale, and he appears to be trembling – yes, she notes that the sword tip is wobbling, causing droplets of blood to fall unevenly onto the stage.

I don't care why you're doing this. I will see you dead for this. The thought warms her, even as she feels the numbness in her face, blood drained away by what she's seen. As if in sympathy.

He licks his lips twice, swallows. His voice is dusty and cracked as he asks, "Chris? You still with me?"

Deborah doesn't hear a reply, but the man reacts as though he's gotten one.

"Good. You need to cover the door now. Someone will probably report the shots."

He smiles, a sick and pathetic thing, turning his face into a mask. *He looks ill*, thinks Deborah, *like whatever's going on inside is finally revealing itself, pushing forward from underneath.*

She thinks fleetingly about her own legs and their sudden inexplicable will to motion, and a connection dances just out of reach before evaporating.

"We're going to have company."

Bad enough we're going to be killed by a lunatic with a bomb, we have to put up with crap B-movie dialogue too?

"No! Don't open it to look. Just be ready if anyone comes in."

She hears a mumbled reply that was probably 'okay'.

The young man addresses the congregation again, and while he regains that volume from before, he sounds like a different person to Deborah. She can feel the toll this is taking on the congregation. She realises, with rising disgust, that she can smell it. But she also realises in this moment that it is, in some non-metaphorical way, also killing *him*. He'd started so strongly, she remembers her conversation with him, her frustration and fear at how smug he'd been, how in control. But now...

Now we're off script. Now, anything goes. Deborah has time to wonder why this should be scarier, and she figures it out: because the script gave them time. Time to pray. Time for the miracle. Now, though, there are four bodies, and a woman on the front row who sounds like she's going to give birth any minute.

Not to mention a cripple who feels sure that, with just a bit more time, she may be able to walk.

Fuck, anything could happen, and the trouble with that is, most of those happenings lead to a premature detonation and an end to the whole mess. And Deborah doesn't want that.

Deborah wants to live. She wants to walk out of here and never look back.

"I want you all to think about what you've seen here. Think about what it might mean. God has a plan. This we are told. God has a plan. This is all part of it. Right? That's what you have to believe. If you believe, this is what you have to..." He trails off. *You look so small*, thinks Deborah. *So ill.* She hates him so much; she feels a little ill herself. Her left foot moves forward, sliding just a little on the step. Her foot is now half off; toes suspended in the air.

That's when he looks over to her, sword swinging around to point, it seems to Deborah, at her face. "'Get behind him?' Deborah? Did you really say that?"

Jonah

Deborah feels a chill run through her whole body.

"Get behind him."

He takes a step towards her. The blade moves a step closer. She stares at it, focussed on the beads of Mike's blood she can see on the tip. She is dimly aware of her heart squeezing in her chest, too fast, painful.

"Get. Behind. Him."

Each word a step. He's near the edge of the stage now, the point of the blade close enough that Deborah feels like she's going to go cross-eyed, but still she can't stop staring.

I'm going to die. He's going to kill me.

"Deborah? Look at me."

She can't. All she can see is the blade, Mike's execution, the blood rising from his neck, the fountain, the dullness in his eyes...

The point jabs forwards, scary close to her face, and she blinks hard, and her eyes refocus on the pale, angry features behind the blade.

His lips are twisted in a snarl. His neck cords stand out like wires under the skin.

I'm going to die.

She feels her anger drain away, recede. She feels herself breathe in, and out. It feels like communion. Like communion used to feel, before the accident turned it into an empty ritual of desperate begging, of unanswered pleas for charity.

It feels real.

This is my breath.

"Deborah."

"Yes." Her voice comes out clear. She is pleased. She wants her last words to be heard, understood.

She takes another breath.

He turns the blade, but she does not look away from his face. *That's where I live or die. In whatever lives behind that strange, angry mask. Eyes on the prize.*

"Get behind him?"

What is he asking? What can she say?

"You think the chair will spare you? Stay my hand?"

"No."

She takes another breath.

"Will you scream?"

He lets the question hang. So does she.

"When I slice open your stomach?"

"Yes."

Trying to divine the question behind the question. *Am I dead? Is there hope?*

She remembers an eternity ago, thinking about free will. She can feel her left leg, out of place but still useless.

She breathes in. She breathes out.

He squats, squinting, reading her face, she thinks, trying to.

"You don't seem scared."

"Maybe I'm terrified." She feels tears trying to rise, chokes them back. She will die with dry eyes. That is her will.

She breathes in. She breathes out. The air is sweet.

He stares at her, eyes vacant. His frown deepens, then locks. He is still panting from the fight, the blood from his nose still drying on his lips. She stares at that for a moment, wondering if she will live to see him wipe his face.

Either I die staring at that bloody nose or I live long enough to see him cleaned up. Win-win, really.

The laugh tickles her diaphragm, threatening to roll out her mouth. For the first time since he turned to her, she feels a stab of terror in her chest. *Not like this.*

She screws her lips together, bites down on her tongue, the pain suppressing the giggle, forcing her to wince.

His eyes regain focus.

She inhales.

"You know what I think?"

"No." She exhales. The urge to laugh is gone. So is the fear. She wants to live. She feels like every cell in her is screaming it.

He allows the silence to hold. The blade points at her chest.

"I think you want me to end it."

"No..."

"I think you've had enough, Deborah."

"No, No, I..."

He jabs forward with the sword. The point pushes against the fabric of her shirt. She feels her skin dimple under the pressure.

"I am talking. You can't lie to me, remember?"

She does not breathe.

"I think you know you're going to die today, and you've decided to do it on your terms. I think..."

She starts to shake her head, feeling the tears rising, and now the struggle to hold them down is too much, and the point of the blade is at her throat, and she goes rigid, body and mind frozen.

"I think you want to commit suicide by sword."

She feels the cold metal on her windpipe. Her mouth is dry. She cannot swallow. Cannot speak. She feels her life twisting by a thin, fine thread. She breathes in shallowly through her nose. She waits.

He leans forward. For a second, she feels the pressure on her throat increase, then his shoulder and arm shifts. He brings his face close enough to hers that she could lean forward and kiss him.

If she could stand.

He looks at her, stares, eyes blazing now, fully aware, alert.

She breathes in. She breathes out. She stares back.

He opens his mouth.

"Do you know what the sadist said to the masochist?"

She can't shake her head for fear of cutting her own throat. Can't speak for lack of spit. She tries to answer with her eyes. She stares, frantic, gaze flicking between his eyes. *Please. Please.*

He leans closer. She sees Mike's blood on his cheek — stark against his milk pale skin. Tastes his breath.

"No."

He grins.

The blade is gone, and he stalks back across the stage, taking the centre, staring out into the congregation.

"Pray! I want to talk to him. The hour grows short."

Deborah feels a tremble start inside her, in her spine, her stomach.

The killer looks back at her, into her eyes.

"The hour grows short."

She closes her eyes.

I'm going it fucking kill you, boy. The thought feels calm. Rational.

It feels like a promise.

Revelation (II)

There's a roaring. Pounding. It surrounds her, engulfs her. Boom, boom, boom. Rhythmic. Titanic. Tidal. She is inside a maelstrom, at the heart of the storm, but it is not calm, it is raging, each pulse concussing her, squeezing and exploding. At first it feels constant. Then, gradually, she discerns a rhythm within the chaos. The explosions are paced, even. As she notices this, they start to fade, becoming less violent. Other sensations fade in. There's a second rhythm, a motion. Up and down. Coolness in, warmth out.

Soothing, this, as the pounding fades and localises, becoming situated, no longer all encompassing. It's motion, her motion. Rise and fall. Repeat.

There's a pulling, dizzying sensation which comes and goes. She feels the weight of something pressing in, pressing down. There's a disembodied moan that rises to a yell then fades again.

Nightmarish. Is this a nightmare? She thinks not. In and out.

Breath.

Not dead then.

Dizzying again, like her consciousness is settling back uneasily into her skull, after being... elsewhere. Somewhere dark.

Somewhere blank.

She's aware of light. Her eyes are shut – feel glued shut,

right now – but she's aware of light behind them. On the other side, there is a lighted space.

Her head is still spinning a little, like that time she got really drunk and then had a bong at that party, and she ended up laying out in the field, holding onto the ground to keep from falling off and wondering if the moon was going to stop that ridiculous spinning thing it had going on. Like that, but without the attendant nausea and feelings of incipient divinity that faded once she started heaving her guts up.

She comes back to her own physicality slowly, hesitantly, afraid of what she will find. Something bad has happened. May still be happening. Right now, there's a massive blank spot where her immediate past should be. She only knows it's a dark place.

A bad place.

The grunting and screaming again. The word nightmare reoccurs, and she regards it lovingly but with no real hope. The screaming is real. So is the bad thing. The pink light appears to be fading in, fading up, becoming brighter. Surfacing, she thinks. She's aware of pressure on her stomach, an unyielding rigid surface under her back, a thin layer of sweat that coats her body like she's been dipped in it.

Yuck.

She doesn't much feel like waking up, truth be told, but she's also got a practical streak. She recognises that it's going to happen anyway, so she goes with the process rather than fighting it, reconnecting with the concept of eyes and eyelids, linking the theory to the hardware, and as she feels the connections slot back into place with a couple of flickers, she opens her eyes, slowly.

Above her is a vision. She's probably the same age as Alex, maybe even a year or two younger. She's got brown hair that falls past her shoulder, and a round, warm face – red cheeks, full lips. Even her chin is cute. She's in profile, so Alex can only see a single bright blue eye, framed by dark lashes, untainted by makeup. The button nose completes the set, thinks Alex. This girl is breathtakingly beautiful.

Alex's eyes go back to the girl's arms, noticing that they are bare. The girl is wearing a no-sleeve vest over a fairly serious set of breasts, which combine with the youthful face on just the right side of obscene, thinks Alex, gamely trying to ignore the reddish stains that can only be blood across the front of the shirt, grateful that the angle is too acute for her to have any more than the vaguest peripheral vision of those hands on her stomach.

Because, something bad.

Alex takes her in, marvelling. Her breathing syncing with the rise and fall of the girl's own. That something bad is starting to form, now, a darkened shape in her rear-view mirror, threatening. Alex is hurt.

The girl shifts, leans forward again, and Alex feels a momentary throb of pain deep in her guts. Just a single pulse, but it drives the breath out of her, forces tears to her eyes. She blinks hard to clear her vision, and sees a small silver cross swing out from the girl's cleavage, dangling free. In her mind, Alex sees the cross above the stage, the dickhead with the bomb and the blade, remembers the punch in the back and the explosion.

Oh. Right.

The flare of pain recedes, but there's a deep rooted throb that remains, still pulsing in time with her heart. Worse is the oozing feeling down there, the feeling of each pulse sending warmth out of her, into the world. *You can't move heat from the cooler to the hotter,* she thinks randomly, *you can try if you want, but you'd far better notta, fucking thermodynamics.*

Still, the girl is bloody lovely. Might as well make conversation.

She draws a couple of more breaths, experimentally, again re-engaging with the mechanics of the process; tongue and lips and breath (oh my).

"Nice chest. I mean, vest."

The girl yelps with shock, body flinching back and away, and again there's a moment of pressure relief before it returns, and this time the pain moves from a snarl to a low growl, and Alex has to pant for breath, too shocked to cry out. Nevertheless, Alex is smiling. Grinning, in fact, as the pressure comes back, and the pain drops away.

Oh yeah. I still got it.

The girl's face turns fully towards her, and Alex notes with little surprise that she's just as beautiful in portrait as she was in profile. Maybe even more.

She's also scowling. Alex allows the grin to relax into a smile, trying to keep out the strain. She licks her lips, trying to get her spit flowing again.

"Come on, that's not bad, considering the circumstances. Pretty sharp."

The smile raises first. Then the frown begins to fade. It's an odd transition; the pacing is off, but Alex is forced again to reflect on the beauty in this face. There's even a dimple in her left cheek, for crying out loud. Just her left cheek. It's borderline unreasonable.

"If you say so."

Her voice is soft, admirably calm, thinks Alex. The words sound so lovely, shaped by that smile.

"I do say so."

Those clear blue eyes hold her own captive, frank and open and caring. Alex holds the look as long as she can, but she's drawn back to her cheek, her ears, her lips, that ridiculously cute dimpled chin. She knows she's being inappropriate, even rude, but Alex feels that, under the circumstances, she's allowed to not give a fuck.

Life's too short.

Alex's eyes do return to the girl's, and she realises that the girl has just been staring right back the whole time. The realisation makes Alex feel giddy, but it's like the opposite of the swimmy feelings she had as she was waking up.

Say something, for fuck's sake.
"So, are you my nurse?"
Role-play Alex? Are you mad? Never on a first date...
"Yes, if you want. I mean, I'm not really..."

Alex shakes her head, making a pfffft noise. *Lord, thanks for sending me this one. You'll make a believer out of me yet, gunshot wound or no gunshot wound.* That light-headed feeling is back, a weird kind of elation, floaty. Alex is carried on it, exuberant.

"Good enough for me. Can't imagine the ones you get on the NHS would do a strip tease just to cheer me up. I like you better."

The girl flushes at this, right down to her roots, turning an alarming brick shade of red, and Alex is slammed by a rapid series of revelations, intuition heightened by adrenaline and the diamond clarity that comes when you understand that your life may be measured now in breaths, in minutes, but almost certainly not in hours.

She sees this girl. Sees her loneliness, her vulnerability. Sees the cross in her mind's eye, and puts it together with the revival nonsense and the plain vest and the fierce blush and the undecorated beauty and the easy, friendly smile, the borderline spectacular breasts, and the tone of her voice and a thousand other noticed unnoticed subtleties, and what she sees is:

- This girl may never have been kissed. She's certainly never been seriously flirted with – or at least, not the right way, a good way. Is there some spotty dickhead with wandering hands lurking somewhere in the background? One who saw those breasts and simply had to grip them, jerk off fodder for months? Oh yeah, almost certainly. And maybe the odd crude comment on the way past in a school hall. But no-one has ever caressed them, lovingly. These breasts are criminally unnuzzled.

- This girl is repressed enough that she doesn't even realise that she might like other girls. Well, she does, on some level - *we all do know,* thinks Alex, *deep enough down* - but it's not something she's spent any serious time thinking about. Dreaming about, maybe, but not thinking about. Banjo country like this, the small silver cross of the believer-by-default, girls kissing girls is just not a thing. Probably not in a 'oh-how-sinful' way so much as a 'completely-outside-of-anything-that-is-thought-about-or-discussed' kind of way. This girl may never have allowed herself to think consciously about whether or not she likes other girls.
- This girl likes other girls. At least, she likes the other girl whose stomach she is holding together, which is why she's smiling like her face is going to split, even as she turns practically puce with embarrassment. *Good for you girl*, thinks Alex. *Better late than never.*

The smile gives way to a chuckle that Alex finds delightful. Even though the girl is looking away, Alex can see a sparkle in her eyes, and Alex feels another wave of something warm spreading from her stomach to the tip of her head, and for a precious second, neither young woman is thinking about bombs or blades or bullets or death, or anything except the pure wonder of each other.

Alex laughs, just a dry huffing sound. It's enough to trigger a wave of pain across her stomach, under her diaphragm, a dark ripping feeling, and this time she can't keep the grimace, the clench, off of her face.

"Jesus, don't make me laugh, please."

"I'm not the one cracking jokes, am I?" Her voice is strained, like she's really angry, but Alex thinks it's just stress talking. They had a little moment, and now the shitty world with its shitty pain and misery is back in the conversation, all elbows.

Still, play nice.

"Sorry, nurse."

The smile flares again. Good.

Alex allows her eyes to go to the ceiling; her head to lie flush against the floor. She feels both cold and sweaty, which is probably not a good thing. She can hear harsh, heavy breathing to her right, presumably from the woman who wins the 'most-unusual-labour-story' prize in her antenatal class. Alongside the 'scariest-moment' award and a special lifetime 'above-and-beyond-the-call-of-trauma' for chronic overachievement in the field of shitty luck.

Other than that, things are pretty quiet. There's some sobbing, mostly of the near-silent variety, and a lot of breathing. To Alex it feels like the whole room is sighing, like a musical round without words or tune. For a moment it feels to her like she could float on it – just rise up and drift into the rafters, through the roof, into the sky, up into the light, away from pain and fear...

She blinks rapidly, trying to come back. It helps, a little, but she's really light-headed now, and that floaty feeling recedes but does not entirely dissipate. Alex suspects she's stuck with it, and she feels the shadow that lurks behind that thought, and for the first time, she shivers.

Her focus shifts back to her blue eyed beauty, her angel. Her face shows concern and fear. And affection. Unmistakable. Alex feels a spike of rage at the realisation. *No fucking time.*

"What time is it?"

The girl looks up and away, at the clock hanging over the door. "Quarter past three."

Shit.

"Wow."

"Yeah. I really didn't think... I mean, I didn't expect, um..."

"Hey, sometimes I surprise myself."

Again Alex smiles, and again she sees the smile answered, but there's sadness there this time, and she thinks this girl sees the shadow too.

"What's your name?"

"Katie. I'm Katie."

"Pleased to meet you, Katie. I'm Alex." Alex raises her arm, faintly surprised that she still can, and is delighted and a little shocked by the warmth she feels as Katie's hand holds her own, gripping gently.

The touch hums with gentle energy, and any lingering doubts in Alex's mind are dispelled. She sees Katie's pupils dilate, that magnificent bosom hitch in a deeper breath. Alex can smell soap on her skin over the sweat of her fear and the background smell of urine that now surrounds them like an overused toilet in a dirty pub.

Beautiful. She is so, so beautiful. Alex feels again a surge that fills out her chest and stomach, and Alex notices the feeling stops there, does not spread across her hips, or into her thighs. Alex understands for the first time that all sensation from the waist down is lost to her – not even a numbness, just a total absence of feeling – comprehends what this must mean, the understanding clear and bright and cold and hard, but still she marvels at how she feels, at this wonderful stranger who is filling her up with a pretty smile.

Katie.

"Wow."

"Wow." Katie agrees. The smile is fucking glowing on her face, and as her fingers trace circles in Alex's palm, Alex has time to think *take me now, Lord. It doesn't get better, so just take me now.*

Then the contact is broken, and the hand returns to her abdomen. Alex feels the pressure down there increase again, and for a second there are spots in front of her eyes and a sickening wave of pain that makes the world go grey, before the colour bleeds back in.

"Fuck!"

"Sorry!"

"Don't. Don't ever. Apologise."

They stay that way for a while, Katie looking at Alex, Alex looking at Katie. Eyes you could dive into, swim around in. Alex feels this, sees it, and feels herself pulling away as she falls forwards. It's wonderful, but it's all wrong too, because Alex is feeling colder and colder, and she knows that the pulling away is not part of the good thing but part of the bad. The sensations are getting dangerously mixed in her mind as the edges of everything become blurry and indistinct. Alex has always hated being cold, and she's infuriated that it's going to be the last thing she feels, and she shivers again, a shudder this time, and the ripples across her abdomen make her cry out.

Katie's face contorts, in sadness and reflected pain. She looks around, frantically, and Alex is sad because she doesn't want Katie to look away, she wants – she needs – Katie's eyes on her. Alex thinks she can deal with whatever comes next, just about, if she's holding that look when it happens.

She's about to speak, to call Katie back to her, but Katie thoughtfully saves her the trouble by turning back herself.

"It's okay. Katie, it's okay."

"No, it isn't! It is not! You need..."

"Katie."

Alex raises her arm again, palm flat, dismayed to discover how heavy it's grown since she last did this. Stop.

Katie does. Her eyes are moist though, and her lower lip is trembling.

"No time? Okay? No time."

Katie starts to shake her head, in mute rejection, tears now starting to fall. Alex wishes distractedly that she could sit up and kiss those tears away.

No time.

"Katie? Do you hear me?"

A sob. Then, "Yes, I do."

"Take my hand."

There's a moment's hesitation as desire wars with fear and duty, and Alex is cheered beyond measure when desire wins. The pressure on her stomach lessens again as Katie's hand returns to her own. She sees red in her peripheral vision as Katie's hand passes through her field of sight. She feels that awful drawing back, that draining sensation, each heartbeat seeming to push her further away, but that beautifully warm hand is back in her own, and the glow with it warms her in ways that the encroaching cold can't touch.

This is it, thinks Alex, as the pain in her abdomen begins to catch fire again. *Find the fucking words.*

"Katie, you..."

"You can kiss me if you want."

The tears are still fresh on her cheeks, her eyes are gleaming, but her voice is calm and steady. Alex feels her mouth fill with water. No longer trusting herself to talk, she nods instead, and Katie brings her face down, and their lips meet.

It is delicate at first, tender, lips almost resting against each other. It's beautiful. Alex gets the faintest taste/smell of strawberry lip balm, and it tastes like childhood sweeties in paper bags. She tries to raise her head to push closer, but it's too hard, too much effort. Katie feels the attempt and pushes forward herself, mouth beginning to open under the pressure. Alex feels those amazing breasts pressing against her, and raises her free right hand to hold, to caress. She feels more of that warmth, that heat, the firmness of the swell, the faint rubbing of a hard nipple poking through layers of fabric against her palm, and Alex is transported, in heaven.

Katie's hand leaves hers and takes hold of the hand over her breast. For a moment Alex thinks she is being rebuffed, then Katie plunges that hand up under her T-shirt and beneath her bra and clenches it into the warm flesh of her breast, squeezing, and at the same moment, her mouth opens fully, and their tongues meet and their teeth clash as they push into each other, tongues dancing, lapping, warm spit flowing, eyes screwed shut, creating a wet warm space of sensation to live in. Their mouths tingle with the heat and intimacy of the kiss. Alex feels as though her hand is burning, branded by the shape of Katie's breast and the nipple now pressed deep into her skin, and she can feel her heart hammering in her chest now, and each pulse sends her just a little further away, a little closer to the darkness and the cold, but Alex gives not a single solitary shit, only wishing this be the last thing she knows, because she thinks right now it was worth every fucking second and indignity and horror and pain, because she's finally kissing a girl the way she always dreamed she would but never had, and she's finally found something that she'd began to dismiss as fiction, something that makes all other encounters she'd had out to be the palest imitation.

Then the moaning starts again, maddeningly close, and for a few precious seconds they both try and ignore it, to just hunker down and live inside the space they've created between their mouths, in the meeting of their tongues, but of course the noise grows, and the pain and the fear are too clear and too unmistakable, and both feel the intrusion, and gradually Katie draws back, and Alex does not try and fight it, even though she feels the loss bitterly. Alex allows herself a split second to hate the pregnant woman and her fucking kid with the fire of a thousand suns, and then opens her eyes.

Or at least tries to. They won't open. She tries to figure out why they won't open, and then realises with a spike of fear that she can't remember how to. The memory of that particular muscle function is gone, and darkness is all she has left. She tries frantically to recall how, willing her eyes to open (ah, but even that impulse, the panic, is growing faint, indistinct, mushy) desperate to see those blue eyes again, but while the memory of sight remains, the part of motor control is simply... absent. Erased. This should terrify her; she wants to be terrified, in point of fact, but she finds herself merely regarding the information, noting the fact of it, assimilating it. It doesn't seem to matter much.

Nothing seems to matter much.

She's aware that she still has a warm, firm breast in her right hand, though it feels like that hand is a mile or so away, the signal coming from a tin can on the end of a long piece of string, and that there's a heart beating hard enough behind it that she can feel the tremors right across her palm. That somewhere someone's moaning (*lord, kum by ya*), but that's it for external signal – otherwise, she may as well be floating in space.

Slipping. Falling, away and out. The glow from the other side of her unresponsive eyelids is fading, the sun setting, the light bulb grows dim, the warmth in her hand also seeming to fall away. The anger flares one final time, a ghost of its former life altering self, a guttering candle flame in what used to be her stomach and is now just another dark place.

She hears her name, faintly, close yet impossibly distant, a phone call from the far side of the moon. She tries to smile, but doesn't know if she's succeeding.

There's more moaning, and then a male voice, yelling with an urgency that feels alien to her,

"I think someone's coming!"

Alex smiles inside and tries to formulate a smart ass response, pulling the words together.

She is still thinking about the sentence when she dies.

Daniel

Andrew looks over at John, hand resting on the open door of their car.

"Are you coming?"

John blinks slowly, turning his head like a lizard too long in the sun. *Four in the afternoon and the fat fuck is still sweating out last night's cider, what a fucking disgrace,* thinks Andrew. *Shithead's probably over the limit right now, driving the fucking car. Fucking embarrassment to the uniform.*

"What do you need me for?" Whiney. Petulant. That weird nasal quality, like his nose is permanently blocked, along with a gross phlegmy rattle.

Lazy fucking shit.

Andrew runs through the conversation in his head — unknown situation, possible missing persons, last known location, SOP, and tires himself out just thinking about it.

"You know what? I don't. You just sit tight, okay? Back in a minute."

John smiles, a tight piggy expression of satisfaction on his face, and Andrew feels a wave of loathing.

"Okay."

Andrew shuts the car door just a little harder than might be strictly necessary, and pulls his hat on. It's been sat on the dashboard most of the day, the black felt soaking up the summer heat like a sponge, and he feels beads of sweat pop on his forehead. He walks towards the community hall, squeezing between parked cars at the pavement, noting the distance of the building from the surrounding houses – *fucking lot of cars on the street, could do with some residents' parking or something, ridiculous* – and reaches the heavy wooden door.

He thinks about calling his location into Control, but John's laziness is still grating on him, like a painful rash.

Fuck it. Let that fat fuck call it in. It's his fucking job, let him do it for a change.

The doors are big, solid wood, no window. The service or whatever should have finished by twelve, and Katie Jennings' parents decided that three hours was too late. So here Andrew is, chasing down a sixteen year old that's probably just on the piss down the mound with her mates or snogging some spotty tosspot on a bench somewhere, and sure, same old same old, but fucking hell, what a way to spend Sunday afternoon. Andrew takes a second to think about what he'd rather be doing - more precisely, *who* he'd rather be doing, and the room he'd rather be doing it in - but it's an unprofitable line of thought, and the trousers he's wearing would make a hard-on uncomfortable, so he shuts it down and gives the door a cursory shake, already sure that it's locked.

It's open.

Andrew takes a step back, momentarily spooked by the way the door just swings open, and his hand pulls it shut again before he can see in.

Shit.

He looks back to the car, intending to make eye contact with John. Hoping John wasn't looking, didn't see him jump, but of course John is 'resting his eyes', looking for all the world like a slightly tanned Jabba the fucking Hutt sleeping off another slave dancing party. Andrew feels another surge of rage.

Lazy cunt.

Fuck him.

Andrew turns back to the door, pushes it open and steps in, mouth moving into place to form the word

'Hello'.

The windows in the room are high but large, which means that although he's stepping out of direct sunlight, the room is well lit, so it's not really that his eyes are having trouble adjusting to the gloom. It's more that his brain is having trouble adjusting to the signal received from his eyes, his ears, his nose.

The room is full. People sit in pews, huddled. Praying? Andrew is not a bad copper, and he has a pretty sensitive antenna for both bullshit and danger. But too much is wrong here, all at once, and the room of silent people feels like a wall of noise - a screaming warning so jagged that it locks him in place. The door swings shut behind him as he takes in the bodies in the aisle, the blood on the floor. Eyes moving up, too slowly, to the girl near the foot of the stage, head lowered over another body. He doesn't even hear the door come to rest behind him as he takes in the blood-soaked figure on the stage that looks like something out of one of those shitty martial arts movies his dad was obsessed with when he was little, and his peripheral vision is pretty sharp but his reactions are dull, rusted by too many soft beats and known drunks and easy pickings and petty vandalism, so even as his eyes widen with shock as he takes in the carnage on the stage, he notices movement to his extreme left, almost senses it, but his eyes and head have barely begun to turn when he hears a sound that roots him to the spot.

Snick.

"Don't."

One word, but the adrenaline is pumping now, now it's too fucking late and he's caught like a rabbit in a snare. His brain is all about the information now, giving him 'shaky voiced perp, terrified, young, male, been crying or yelling', giving him 'that's gunpowder you can smell over the piss you can also now smell', giving him 'that window at the back above the blood-soaked stage is broken, that body in the aisle looks shot'.

So it's not exactly a surprise to him that the barrel that's pressed into the cheek below his left eye is still transmitting a low heat, not dissimilar to the uncomfortable warmth of his hat. All in all, it's not exactly welcome information either, because a)it's about three seconds too late to be any practical use, and there's very little worse than working out how and why something has gone spectacularly bad after it's too fucking late to do anything about it, and b) one thing that *is* worse is having a scared teenager who has already shot at least one person in the last couple of hours literally pushing a gun into your face.

Andrew runs hot and cold. He feels faint and sick, and his muscles lock up as everything goes as still as it possibly can. Andrew feels a dreadful pulling in. For a few moments his vision itself becomes tunnelled, acid bubbling up from his gut towards his throat, but he could no more vomit right now than he could burst into song. His gullet is in lockdown. Sweat coats his entire body surface, like a second skin, slick against his clothes. He feels it soaking in, his underwear adhering to him.

He draws in breath slow and shallow through his nose, because even though his mouth is still open, still frozen in the act of forming that moronic greeting beloved of sheep before the slaughter everywhere, his tongue appears to have swollen to the size of a tennis ball and is about as dry. It sits in his mouth, blocking the airway, as useless as the rest of him.

Andrew stands, breathes. His life does not flash before his eyes. Time does not seem to slow, exactly, though he feels aware of each inhale and exhale on a level he would not before this moment have even suspected could be possible. What does occupy his mental processing, blotting out all other thought like a total eclipse, is the simple concept of pounds per square inch, and how many more of them stand between him and oblivion.

The finger that will make that determination is

trembling. Andrew knows this because he can feel the tremble transmitted through the warm metal pressed into his face, jittering against his cheek, almost painful because his facial muscles are as taut as the rest. It seems to Andrew like that tremble is going right into his brain, shaking, rattling, and how many pounds per square inch? How big of a twitch will it take? How big a clench of that trigger finger?

Will he even hear the bang?

Time does not seem to slow, but Andrew feels like he's getting older a lot quicker, all of a sudden. Like something vital is leaving him with every out breath.

His whole mind, all of his attention is tuned to that transmitted tremble, so it takes his brain a couple of seconds to realise what his staring, unblinking eyes are seeing.

Which is movement.

The figure on the stage - who was kneeling, Andrew realises, mind replaying what he's been looking at while his attention has been absent in the land of the twitching gun hand where Every Tremble Feels Like The End - climbs to his feet. It takes him a moment, and at first Andrew thinks the man must be old, or at least middle aged. Then he sees, no, it's just a kid, a very pale, extremely crazy looking kid, who has a sword in one hand and something else in the other and a chest covered in crazy wiring that Andrew would dearly like to imagine is some kind of dumb prop or extreme fashion statement. But there's a warm gun pushing into his face and blood everywhere (including all over this pale fucker and the fucking *sword* he's got in his fist) and yup, that's another body on the stage, fucking butchered, looks like, so we're in a cosy quadruple murder with at least two suspects, seventy odd hostages, and we're hoping that the one with the sword just has on a *pretend* bomb vest?

Andrew does not think he's having that kind of luck today. Maybe not ever again.

The kid is looking at him, and his face looks drawn, and *really* fucking pale, though Andrew supposes that the blood spatters on his face might be exacerbating the effect. His eyes look sunken and red, but Andrew thinks what he's seeing is concern. Maybe even compassion. It's a pretty unlikely expression, given the overall picture, and something about it makes Andrew feel... not fear, but something deeper, more elemental. Like the deep moorings of his mind are being put under strain, just by proximity to the madness of another. Andrew sees a killer staring at him with all the appearance of sympathy, and feels a light-headed dread flood into his mind, like white smoke from green wood.

"Chris."

The voice is a little rough sounding but plenty loud enough – it carries across the room with ease. Andrew feels the gun barrel push into his cheek harder, suddenly. He also feels his own awful impulse to pull away squeezed out by an even stronger desire to stand fucking still, and the conflict feels physical to him, even though he does not so much as flinch. The pressure stiffens, then goes back to shaking, maybe a little worse than before, and for the first time in his life, Andrew understands the mechanism whereby someone might just wet themselves with fear. He's been in the car for two hours, and he's got a pretty good bladder capacity, but it's a hot day and now there's this pressure, and this horrible desire to loosen and just let. It. Go.

Please don't kill me. Please calm down and please don't kill me.

"Chris."

Less of a reaction this time. The trembles subsiding a little. Andrew catches up to the fact that the killer on the stage is looking past him, not at him. That the care on his face is meant for his accomplice - *the submissive one*, thinks Andrew, using *a gun instead of a blade, scared*. He feels his mind settle back into place, and for the first time since he heard the sound of metal sliding into place by his left ear,

Andrew feels a small space open in his mind for thought. It's like the realisation about the killer has reminded him *how* to think, like his brain had slipped into neutral, and he's just gotten the bite back.

"Be calm, Chris. Be calm." *Listen to the nice man, Chris. For fuck's sake, please...*

Andrew hears a sob. Feels it, as it rolls up the arm of the shooter and through the barrel into his face. It is a desperate and terrible sound, and Andrew blinks hard, involuntarily, and is kind of amazed when his eyes open and the world is still there.

"Chris..."

"Stop it! Just stop!"

The guy on the stage makes an odd gesture, moving his arms up and down slowly in a way that might look more calming if the hands doing it did not contain a bloodstained blade and a lump of plastic with wire coming out. Similar problem with the bloody pale face and the wrinkled forehead of concern, the slowly shaking head.

"It's okay, Chris. It's okay."

"What the FUCK are you talking about?"

On the word fuck, the barrel of the gun is driven into Andrew's face hard enough to prang his cheekbone. He feels a little burst of pain, and has to clench hard to keep his bladder from emptying.

"What the FUCK is okay?"

This time the barrel moves back before coming forward, and Andrew's head rocks a little. It's like being punched. He feels water squirt into his eye. The pain overrides the fear though, with its immediacy, so he doesn't feel like pissing again. He does start breathing a little heavier though, aware of this but unable to control it. He's sweating so hard now it fucking hurts. His heart doesn't feel like it's beating faster, but it does feel like it's beating pretty fucking *heavy*. Andrew thinks in a desperately distracted way that this cannot possibly be good for him.

"It's the plan, Chris. Remember?"

This time the gun arm freezes completely, the barrel less than a centimetre from Andrew's cheek. He's still staring straight ahead, at the bladed killer with the smooth line in patter, but there's a huge grey lump in his peripheral vision with a dark pit in the centre that seems to Andrew to be roughly the size of the Blackwall tunnel.

"It has to be the plan. Okay? This whole thing. Him too."

The blade points at Andrew here, marking him out, but the gaze of the kid doesn't shift for a second. He's clearly holding his focus where it needs to be, like a fucking snake hypnotising its master. Andrew knows he's got the power relationship right, but can also see that the situation is what we like to call fluid, and there's panic up front as well as behind, for all the calming voice and soothing gestures and let's-be-reasonable words, and Andrew feels something very dark and unpleasant begin to bloom in his heavily beating chest.

"Come on, Chris. You know it."

"I don't, I fucking..."

That big black hole is floating about now, and it's like a fly that's buzzing around your face too close to properly focus on, only knowing the fucking thing could end you in less than a second, and Andrew's still not feeling afraid, exactly, but that dark feeling is growing.

"Yes." There's a smile here, which in Andrew's humble opinion is spectacularly ill-judged, because the face on the stage is not well suited to smiling at the best of times, and these are kind of the opposite of the best of times.

But it must be working, because Chris stops talking. Which Andrew approves of, because the tremble in the arm was in the voice too, which indicates a level of pressure and a lack of control that are spectacularly ill-suited to the error-free operation of a firearm.

"You do know, Chris. You've always known. The way I haven't. The way I need to. You *know*."

His voice lowers in pitch as he delivers the last word,

and he takes a step forward, reaching the edge of the stage.

Andrew hears Chris draw breath, as if to speak. Hold it, exhale. Once. Twice. The kid on the stage nods his head, slowly.

"That's why this is going to work, right?"

There's another hitch of breath, and to Andrew it sounds damp, like a sob, but that dark feeling is not moving and Andrew is convinced on a molecular level that any movement would be a supremely bad idea, so he does not check, does not even move his eyes in that direction.

The silence drags, spins out, ragged breaths, the boy on stage nodding, then there's a shuffling noise from behind him and the gun recedes in his peripheral vision, becoming gun sized rather than planet sized. It should be a relief, but Andrew actually feels a very edgy jag, because it's not far enough back to make any difference. The angle is still wrong for him to try and chance a poor reaction time and the fucking thing is still there and still cocked.

The kid on the stage holds the silence for a few moments longer, then his eyes shift slightly, and now Andrew knows he's being appraised for the first time. Andrew stares back, careful to keep his face neutral, but also determined to hold his gaze. Andrew feels the eyes of everyone in the room on him for the first time, and the unwelcome responsibilities of the uniform flood back into him. He can feel just as scared as he likes, but he'd better not show it, because these people are looking to him. This is the job.

So he can't stop the bead of sweat that he can feel rolling from the hollow of his left temple down the side of his face, but he can damn well keep his eyes front and centre. There's a relief to this too, this assumption of a role - one he knows well, has played with reasonable success for years. He remembers training, being told *most of the time; the uniform is worth an army by itself*, and hasn't he seen it, time after time? *Yup, affirmative.*

So he's being sized up. The kid on the stage imagines

himself tough, but it's clear to Andrew that he's pushed himself way past any place of comfort. That maybe the barbecue doesn't taste quite as good as he'd thought it would. Is, in point of fact, making him ill. The kid is so fucking pale, drawn. There are shadows under his eyes, and even across the length of the hall, Andrew can see they are bloodshot. Still, the kid is alert, and...

"Officer?"

"Yes." Andrew is pleased with how calm his voice sounds. His heart still feels like it's beating too hard, but the dark feeling has... not receded, exactly, but been balanced out by the counterweight of what Andrew thinks of, without irony or self-consciousness, as his duty.

"What happens now?"

The question feels like it should throw Andrew, but somehow it doesn't.

"Well, Control knows my last known location is here," *Unless my lazy sack of shit partner is still dozing in the car,* "so they'll be expecting to hear from me in the next five minutes max. To confirm the location is empty."

"I see." The kid nods, and Andrew thinks the gears are still spinning, but he couldn't swear to it.

"I take if they don't hear from you, they'll send more?"

"That's right, yes. A lot more, probably." Is that laying it on too thick? Maybe, but only a little. They *should* send all units within ten minutes of an officer not responding, even in this chicken-shit outfit, *if* John has called it in, *if* John doesn't get curious and just tries to come on up here himself, *if...*

"That would be inconvenient, Officer." There's an edge inside that voice that Andrew dislikes intensely, and dislikes all the more for the ragged quality of it. It's the voice of someone who knows they are out past some fundamental point of no return, but still feels willing to keep on pushing. Come what may.

"May I ask why you are here in the first place?"

Andrew hesitates for a fraction, but can see no angle in

lying.

"Responding to a Missing Persons. The parents called it in. This is her last known location."

Even as he's saying this last, Andrew is wincing inside. *Too much information, idiot! Don't need to lie, okay, but have some fucking restraint.*

"I see. Chris?"

Andrew sees the kid's focus shift behind him, then shift back.

"So, Officer...?"

Play dumb? But what's the point? The question is clear.

"Officer Jackson. Andrew Jackson."

"Officer Jackson. Would you mind telling us all who it is you've come here looking for?"

Yeah, that's the problem with honesty, reflects Andrew, *you just can't see how it's going to bite you in the balls until it's too fucking late.* Making up a name is out of the question, and Andrew intuits that 'need-to-know' is likely to lead to bloodshed sharpish. Anyway, it's not exactly a state secret, just protocol. Still, it pains him to have to say "Katie Jennings."

Especially when he sees the huddled over figure in the aisle snap to in scared recognition. Andrew's eyes are drawn to the movement, so he sees with unasked for clarity the look of hurt and confusion in the girl's face. Sees too the limp arm fall out from under her shirt, back to the prone figure on the floor. The one down there might just be unconscious, but Andrew thinks more likely deceased. The pain in poor Katie's so-blue eyes is all the confirmation he could ask for.

Shit.

"So, you're Katie?" The blade is pointing down at her, and she stiffens up further, eyes locked onto Andrew's, pleading, desperate. *Don't make me, please don't make me.*

"She fits the description, yes." It feels like the right move. Minimum buys her some time. Maybe more. She's still scared, but he sees relief, gratitude. *Good call, Andrew.*

"And you said her parents called it in."

"That's right. She's sixteen. Should have been home by twelve thirty, so they called it in at three." Telling it feels right too. Buy time with meaningless detail. It helps Andrew feel more in control too, talking like an officer. Doing his job. Humanise the hostages. Make him see them as people.

The kid cocks an eyebrow, and Andrew realises he's looking back at his accomplice. He clearly likes what he sees there, because the smile that comes is smaller but more real.

"Apologies, Officer. You find us in the middle of an experiment, and much has not gone according to plan."

He laughs at this, and to Andrew it's a terrible sound, broken glass grinding in concrete.

"Or maybe it has, after all." The eyes seem blank to Andrew suddenly, opaque, and that dark feeling comes back with a vengeance.

"My friend and I are relieved to see you, let's just leave it at that."

Andrew is desperate to respond, but his mind scrabbles for purchase, unable to find anything to grip onto, and he feels his eyes pulled back to Katie, who is crying, he sees, big blue eyes running freely, silently, her lower lip shaking badly. It twists in Andrew's gut, every protective instinct screaming to do something, but he can't think of a fucking thing to do or say. He looks back at the stage and sees the killer is now staring down at her. He comes within an ace of taking a step forward until he remembers the loaded gun, just out of sight, pointed at the back of his skull. He winces in frustration but holds his place. He watches the kid sit on the edge of the stage; blade pointed at Katie's back. Sees her face again, a mask of misery, but Andrew realises with a start that he sees no fear there at all, only loss. He feels his breath catch in his throat at the realisation, because it's not what he would have expected in a million years. The immediate impact is for him to feel something he hasn't felt since he took that step into the building, lo those many aeons ago.

Still, the darkness is stronger.

The girl holds his eyes, even through the tears. He hopes his face is giving comfort, and decides to stay with her, ignoring the kid. *She's beautiful*, he thinks, *even in her grief she is beautiful*, and he thinks about that hand falling out from under her shirt, what it probably means, and he marvels at what civilians are capable of, for good and ill.

Then he sees the kid's hand appear over her shoulder, come to rest there, and he sees her go still, her eyes darkening. He flicks back to the kid, sees the blade now resting across his thighs as he squats, his face a mixture of eagerness and hunger that turns Andrew's stomach. His eyes flick back to Katie but he's just too slow to hide his own reaction, and she sees it, and he sees despair flood her grief, and Andrew is ashamed of himself.

"Katie." The voice is quieter, softer, but it still carries.

"Yes."

There's a dull quality to her voice that Andrew does not like at all. Resigned. Already half dead.

No good.

The hand rests on her shoulder, leaving blood on her white vest. She does not flinch or try to move away.

"Is he telling the truth, Katie?"

"Yes. I am Katie Jennings. I'm sure Dad is..."

But she can't finish the sentence, lowers her head and sobs instead, and Andrew feels terrible, but he's also glad, because she's reconnecting with her feelings, back to herself. Away, he hopes, from resignation.

The kid nods as though she can see. He even pats her back, in a gesture of comfort that strikes Andrew as obscene. His eyes are still blank, and Andrew imagines the smell of burning.

"That's good. It's good to have people that care for you."

Katie sobs again, an awful high sound, wrenching.

Andrew sees her gaze drop down to the body, hold there.

"Katie. I need to ask you something, okay?"

There's something really shitty about the way he asks for permission, thinks Andrew, and the taste is bitter in his mind. He hates the kid, at this moment.

Katie nods, tears spilling down her cheeks as her head moves.

"Why did you help this person, and not..."

"Alex!"

There's an anger, no, fury in her voice. Andrew likes it a great deal.

"Her name is Alex."

Was, thinks Andrew, but the semantics are not as important as the defiance. *A warrior, or just with her blood up?* Either way, Andrew reckons he's got an ally in this one.

If he can somehow keep her alive.

"I'm sorry," says the kid. Andrew thinks he may mean it. Doesn't help with the hate.

"My question is, why did you help Alex, and not the young man who collapsed earlier? I asked for help, a doctor, and you didn't..."

"I'm not a doctor. I'm not anyone!"

The hell you aren't, thinks Andrew.

"But, you..."

"I WAS SCARED! And then... when she was shot... I couldn't stand it, just being scared. I had to do something."

The kid is soaking it up, and Andrew again sees an awful hunger. The kind that is normally only fed, never satisfied. He's seen it on the face of many of the drunks that grace the cells so often on a Friday and Saturday night in this town. Seen it on a couple of bodies too. The ones who never beat it.

"Katie, are you a believer?"

"Oh, what does it matter?" Andrew sees her forehead wrinkle with frustration.

"Are you?"

"YES! Yes, okay, yes I am."

"And has He.. have you..." The hesitancy is fascinating, awful. Such hunger.

"No. It, I only get a feeling sometimes. That's all. Never words. Just a feeling. When I pray. Sometimes."

"Today?"

"No. Not today."

The kid seems torn by this. Andrew sees a dark satisfaction warring with hope, with that driving need. The kid doesn't seem to know whether to gloat or cry.

"What about when you helped Alex? Then?"

Andrew sees Katie's eyes flash as the name is spoken. And Andrew again thinks this girl has a rage he could really use, if only they get the chance, and he's well satisfied with that.

"No. I felt... No. Not that."

Does the kid understand what's going on here? Andrew thinks not. Andrew thinks the kid does not understand what Katie has been feeling in the last few hours, and Andrew has an insane intuition that that lack of knowledge may just be very costly indeed.

"Thank you, Katie." Patting her back again, distractedly, turning his attention back to Andrew. Andrew feels it like a weight, and he thinks again of his duty, doing the job. It centres him. He realises he's drawing strength from the example Katie has just given him. He's grateful to her.

"Officer Jackson?"

"Yes."

"How long until your silence becomes suspicious?"

"Not long. A few minutes, maybe less." *Unless John decides to break the habit of a lifetime and get off his ass, come knocking. Then there's apt to be shooting.*

The kid nods, appraising. Then he stands, steps past Katie into the aisle, raising his blade to point once more at Andrew.

"Officer, we're seeing signs and portents here.

Significant ones. All may yet be well."

Andrew thinks about the bodies at his feet, the one on the stage, Katie's angry grief. He makes no comment.

"Will you allow us to continue? Uninterrupted?"

Andrew has a pretty good idea about what he's being asked, but if he's right, he needs to play for time, prepare himself.

"What do you want?"

The kid smiles, bloodless and without humour.

"I want a revelation. A miracle. A conversation. But from you, what I mainly want is to radio your friends at the station and tell them that there's nothing going on here, and you're going back out on patrol. I want you to use the radio to... actually, when does your shift end?"

Ten. I'm on the twelve to ten."

The kid takes another step. He's now seven paces away? Six?

"And could you keep sending them messages saying all is well, between now and then?"

Andrew takes his time answering. Partly it's because he's trying to weigh up the honest answer, even though he has no intention of doing as the kid asks - he's learned through his Friday night poker sessions that the best way to deceive someone is to run your mind through the thoughts you would have if you had what you want them to think you have. So he honestly tries to figure out if, hypothetically, he could give control the run-around until he goes off shift at ten, and finally says "I think so, yes. Unless something major kicks off."

It's the truth, and it has the ring. The kid takes three deliberate steps. The blade is fully extended, and the point is now two paces from Andrew's body. Andrew sweats under his stab vest.

The kid's eyes slip away from him, and Andrew hears feet shifting on the floor, and suddenly the gun has moved back into view too big and too close, and Andrew feels that dark feeling erupt in his stomach, blooming, spreading, and his mouth is dry and his mind is suddenly weary.

"Now officer, it's time for the important question. I have a reasonable nose for bullshit, and in my experience people lie worse under stress than normally, so I encourage you to tell the truth. Do you hear me?"

Andrew does not trust himself to speak. He nods. His eyes are now captive to the kid's gaze. It makes him feel light-headed and sick.

"Good. Because if I hear you say anything that I don't like, or that sounds like a code that you no doubt have in place for situations like this..."

You fucking idiot. If you had a clue, you'd be dangerous. Andrew's played enough poker that his face moves not at all as this flashes through his mind, and the kid ploughs on, regardless.

"...Chris here will end you. So my question is – are you going to say anything to give us away?"

It's a gift, the purest grace. Andrew does not smile as he says "no," but it's an effort. Because, no, he's not going to say one word out of place.

You don't need to do that when you press the red button to send the message.

You can say anything, or nothing at all, and every single cop on duty will converge like flies on shit. The location information he'll be giving is the icing on the cake, but even without that, this building will be swarming in ten minutes, tops.

Thank you, God, Andrew thinks, without really thinking at all.

The kid reads Andrew's nervous sincerity just right, apparently, because his arm relaxes and the blade points loosely towards the bodies between them. Andrew holds the kid's eyes steady.

"Good, then. Please, proceed."

Andrew reaches his hand towards his radio, finger already curling to reach behind the main receiver button, in his mind already hitting the red button concealed there. Feeling a swell of simple gratitude so strong it probably looks like fear – gratitude to whatever little nerd genius figured out the perfect place to hide a panic button. He does not try and catch Katie's eye, or move focus away from the kid, but he does send her a last thought, a positive message, *don't be scared, help is coming*, his hand touches the cold black plastic of his radio, and it feels amazingly good in his hand, comforting, the shape of the thing that gets you home safe, and that's when a piercing scream bursts from the front row, incredibly loud and sudden, and it's the last thing Andrew hears.

The last thing he sees is a bright flash to his left, followed immediately by a fierce punch in the cheek.

Then nothing.

Romans

3. 42PM
BARNSTAPLE CONTROL ROOM
EMERGENCY BROADCAST TRANSCRIPT.
SIGNAL BREAKS IN:

[MULTIPLE SCREAMS, INDETERMINATE GENDERS]
]
[MALE VOICE 1, SHOUTING] Fuck. Fuck.
[MALE VOICE 2] (inaudible)
[MALE VOICE 1 (SHOUTING, DISTRESSED)] Fuck
you. Fuck your bullshit. I'm done with it.
[MALE VOICE 2] (closer) Chris...
[CROSSTALK]
[MALE VOICE 1] I'm done. I'm fucking done....
[MALE VOICE 2] Chris, it's part of the
plan...
[MALE VOICE 1] ...I'll fucking shoot you,
you take another fucking step...
[MALE VOICE 2] Okay Chris, calm yourself...
[MALE VOICE 1] Fuck you. You want a plan?
I'm going to count to ten, and then

TRANSCRIPT ENDS

Joel

"I'm going to put a bullet through my own skull, right? Then we'll know, yeah? No more fucking about, no more..."

"...Chris it won't work, you know it won't, it needs..."

"FUCK YOU! Fuck you! I don't give a shit if it works, I just..."

"Officer Jackson, please state your current location. Over."

"Yes you do, Chris. You do. Everything has built to this, don't..."

Chris presses the barrel of the gun to his cheek. The pain is immediate and intense, and he pulls it away with a hiss. The eye above the burned cheek fills with water. He blinks furiously, trying to focus on the bomber.

Chris wants him to see this.

"One!"

"Repeat: Officer Jackson, please." Click.

"You know it won't work, Chris. A man of faith cannot tempt Him, it won't..."

The same bullshit, thinks Chris.

"Two!"

"...work. You will go straight to hell, and none of us will be any the..."

The same arguments they'd had, night after night, trying to design the perfect test. The way to test without testing. A way to prove God, once and for all.

The same bullshit.

"Three!"

"...wiser. Don't forget what this is about. Don't forget..."

The stench – burning, blood, piss and shit. There's no God here. Maybe there never was.

"Four!"

"... what we're trying to achieve. It's cost too much, Chris. Too much..."

Chris thinks about cost. About what the bomber has lost. About his will. About his willingness to give up his own place in heaven, just for the chance to *know*.

Chris thinks about what this has cost him.

"Five!" Voice almost a sob now. Too much. All too much. It should have worked by now, if it was going to. Surely, God knows. Surely, God sees. Surely...

"...for me. Too much for you. You have to see this through. We're so close, can't you feel it?"

Can you feel it? The words the bomber had spoken when he'd shown Chris the vest. Explained how he'd gotten it. Divine provenance. How could it be other? The means to deliver everything they'd discussed, all those other times. The safely hypothetical suddenly brought within their grasp. Real.

Can you feel it?

"Six."

"You can, can't you? I know you can. I can feel it too."

Chris hitches in a breath at this last, the words following with his thoughts, like the bomber had plucked them out of his mind whole. The gun feels heavy in his hand, suddenly. He feels something spark in his stomach.

"I can feel it. I can. This..." blade pointing to the body heaped at Chris' feet, "...is a critical part. I feel it. We're getting close."

"Seven." He says the word hesitantly. Remembering the two of them standing over another body, the night before. The crucified, gutted body of the bomber's father.

Hearing the story of how it had happened. Considering the awful symbolism, the grotesque coincidence, and then seeing the look in his friend's eyes.

Believing. Believing in the reality of the test. Understanding there was finally the means to prove to his friend what he needed so badly to know. Believing that Chris could be a part of it. The crucial part.

"Can you still get your father's gun? Do you know how to use it?"

Back in the present, that same voice:

"We're so close now. This is the desert. Don't you think? This is forty days. This is temptation. This is Gethsemane. We're close, Chris. We're going to see something. I think before nine o'clock, we're going to see miracles."

That conversation, the memory of it realer than all that has passed since.

"I feel it Chris. I do."

"R... Really? You feel it?"

"I do, Chris. I don't know it, but I feel it. I feel like I'm going to get my conversation. And... I feel like you're going to get to see some shit, Chris. And I think you feel it too, don't you?"

Deborah looks at the fallen policeman. She allows herself a moment of frustration. He'd seemed like a useful person, potentially – a missing link, someone who could give her the space she needed to do what she planned to do. Looking at the small hole in his temple, skin blackened around the edge of the wound, she wonders who will replace him.

"I... Yes. I do."

"I know. That's why... this. It's the temptation. We knew it would come. We thought it would be me, but..."

"Yeah. Yes. We did."

"It was you, brother. But you're stronger, aren't you?"

Deborah looks back up at Chris, sees with no surprise that he's crying again, wiping his cheek with his empty hand.

"Apparently. Just."

He laughs, a single, shaky sound. Deborah feels a surge of disgust, but she is well pleased all the same. *He's so fucking weak.* So malleable, she thinks.

The bomber laughs too. Her hate runs cold.

"Okay, well, there's going to be more now, right? Probably a negotiator, something like that. How are we doing for time?"

"Quarter to four."

"Think we can hold them for five hours?"

"If you're doing the talking, we could probably hold them for five weeks."

The bomber laughs again at that, and Deborah has to close her eyes for a second and just breathe deep.

Never mind those two. You know what you need to know about both of them. What you don't know is where your help is coming from. So look, woman. Find your accomplice.

The bomber starts giving orders. One of the central pews to her left is emptied of people, and men from the back rows are ordered to stack the bodies of the priest and the other guy in front of the doors. Deborah's eyes move over the congregation, seeking out someone, anyone, who doesn't look like they've completely given up.

It's hopeless. Hardly anyone is even looking in her direction, and the few that do won't even meet her gaze, eyes sliding away from her as though she were furniture. She realises with rising anger, and not a little fear, that that *is* how they see her – this goddamn beshitted wheelchair has rendered her an object, not a person. Even if anyone was thinking straight enough to realise that the only way out is by taking down the bomber, Deborah is the last person they'd look to for a co-conspirator.

Nobody is going to help her.

She can't do it by herself.

Deborah feels panic start to rise. She feels sweaty, hot. Frantic. She does not want to die in this building, but they are all running out of time. *Someone, one of you, please...*

"Katie?"

Deborah jumps in her chair at the voice. The bomber has moved up the aisle, and is standing now with his back to her. In front of him, Deborah can just make out the girl kneeling, also facing away from the stage. By the other body.

"What do you want?"

Something about her tone makes the hair on the back of Deborah's neck stand up.

"I'm sorry. I need to clear the aisle now. I need you to move Alex."

He has his back to you.

Deborah's heart starts to hammer in her chest. Her mouth goes dry. How far away is he? How many steps?

She places her left foot on the ground. Tests the weight.

"Yes, okay."

It feels solid. Not wobbly.

"Do you... Shall I get someone to help you, or..."

Could she run? Would he hear her? Could Deborah get to the sword before he...

Her thought is interrupted, cut short, as he takes a step back, straightening up. Instinctively, she pulls her leg back, putting her foot back in the cup.

"I'm sorry this happened. I think I would have liked her."

Closer to Deborah, back still to her. But the speed of his movement has spooked her badly, and she turns back instead to face the stage.

Wondering if she'll get another shot.

Katie looks down at Alex, trying to assess how she might move her. Thinks too about hearing her voice. Her own mind, giving her what she wants the most. It should make her feel even worse, but maybe things are so bad that it can't. Maybe going crazy can be comforting.

You're not crazy, just big boned. Now move me, before that asshole hurts you. Do it or...

Or you'll kill me. I know.

Katie cannot help but smile. It makes her look younger than sixteen – makes her look like a child. *I can do this*, she thinks, and is relieved to discover that she really believes it, that it's a statement of fact, not some attempt to gee herself up.

She leans forward over Alex, taking her in.

Her. She's a she. Who knew?

Katie means to remember her like this for the rest of her life, and so she takes her time, eyes cataloguing every detail of her hair, face, skin, body. Her eyes move across that stained purple shirt, the heavy jacket, the bloody cloth still held uselessly to her stomach, and Katie cannot unsee the gaping wound now concealed beneath, knows she will carry that too, right to the end, down to her waist, her..

Katie's breath catches in her throat. The jacket has an inside pocket, at waist height, and there's something in there. Something cylindrical.

Katie is aware that her heart is suddenly beating very hard indeed, that she's all but panting, and her eyes appear to be glued to that shape as her mind, never the sharpest, tries to process this new data.

The pocket isn't where a pocket would normally be. And it's an odd shape. She leans forward just slightly, to get a better look, not thinking about how that might look, curiosity alive and bright. She sees what looks to her like fresh stitching. The fabric that makes up the pocket is leather, but a different kind from the jacket.

Alex made this. She made a hidden pocket in her jacket and put something in there. Katie finds herself reaching out for it, then suddenly snatches her hand back like it touched something hot. *Idiot! Do you want everyone to see you?*

Katie almost looks around, before realising that would look even worse. *If someone has seen, they've seen. Don't get yourself caught now. Calm down. Focus. Get her out of the aisle. Get her somewhere out of sight. Then, maybe, you can see what there is to see.*

She leans forward again and slides an arm up under Alex's armpits. Their faces are close, and Katie can't help but remember the kiss, and her lips tingle slightly at the memory. Then she gets her feet under her and lifts. There's an awful slurping sound as Alex's back peels from the wooden floor and the congealing layer of blood beneath, and Katie feels her stomach flop.

Alex is slim and not tall, but she is horribly slack, and Katie almost drops her at first. She has to thread her hands together behind Alex's back and pull her in, gripping her to her body. She feels Alex's face push into the soft flesh of her chest.

It should feel awful, but somehow it doesn't. *It's what she would have wanted,* thinks Katie, and it feels true enough that she almost smiles again, arms around her dead lover. Katie looks up, sees that the aisle they both came from has cleared, the residents displaced to other pews. She sees sweaty bald man, hovering at the edge of the row behind. He's shifting from foot to foot, frowning. Did the madman say something, before giving Katie her instructions, or did they just move?

Doesn't matter.

Katie begins to shuffle step Alex forwards, the heels of the dead girl stretching out behind her. Four steps in and her heel hits a clotting lump of blood on top of a deeper liquid layer. The combination sends her foot skidding out from under her. She feels the lurch, her centre of gravity fail, but it's too late to do anything, and she lands on her ass with a squelch. The body slides forward as Katie falls, so Katie ends up sitting on Alex's feet, the girl's pale face still buried in Katie's chest. Alex's jacket flies open as they hit the ground, and Katie hears the sound of glass connecting with a hard surface as the jacket slaps the wood. To Katie, it sounds like the loudest noise in the world.

There's an awful silence. Katie wonders if someone is going to laugh, like at school the time she dropped her lunch tray on the way to her table. Katie wonders if the madman heard the glass. Katie wonders what will happen next.

Nothing happens.

Katie leans over, flips the jacket closed, and drags Alex clear of the blood, knees bent, low to the ground. She looks down to make sure she's past the slip zone, then straightens up again, and concentrates on moving until they reach the far edge of the empty row.

Putting Alex down is hard. Katie does not want to lose the intimacy of holding her. She lowers Alex very slowly, gently, one hand cradling the back of her head to stop it hitting the ground hard. Her fingers rest in Alex's hair. It feels delicious. Awful. Katie shudders, tears up.

She slides her hand out from under Alex's head and raises it to her own face, wiping away the fresh tears. She can smell Alex on her fingers, a mixture of shampoo and girl sweat. Katie feels like something is pulling in her mind and feels her chest tighten. She realises she's on the verge of just totally losing it, and that if she does, she's unlikely to be any use to anyone, so she pulls herself together instead. She takes her hand from her face and returns it to Alex, resting against the bulge she can now see clearly in her jacket. She hopes the gesture looks natural.

A hand grabs her wrist.

Numbers

"You really hurt me, you know."

Somehow she manages not to scream. He's kneeling next to her, leaning close enough that, now they are facing, she can see fine dark stubble on his upper lip. His eyes are bloodshot, with big black circles around them. He looks angry, distracted.

The sweaty bald man opens his mouth and says, "When you hit me in the stomach. That really hurt."

"I'm sorry!" It comes out harder than she intends. She's scared, and she's dismayed to realise that fear hasn't left her after all, but it's a distant kind of scared, and behind it is a yawning darkness. *This man is trouble. This could be bad.*

The absurdity of that last almost makes her laugh.

"It hurt." He continued, as though she hadn't spoken. He is looking her in the eyes, but his own eyes seem unfocused. Empty. Katie feels unsteady, like the ground is moving underneath her. "I was just trying to stop you getting killed. You really hurt me." His hand rubs a spot on his belly, eyes never leaving hers. His breath smells to Katie like spoiled milk.

He's still gripping her wrist. Hard.

"I didn't want you to die; that's all. I don't want to die either." He blinks, eyes pulling back to the here and now, focussing on her face. She can see he's very scared, perhaps hysterical. Also, still angry.

147

The swaying feeling increases, and she's almost sure she is moving, but his face hangs constant and steady, so it must just be in her head.

"We're going to though, aren't we? We're going to burn."

"Probably, yes." It falls out of her mouth, but having said it without thinking, she realises she believes it. She'll take whatever she finds in Alex's pocket - if this arsehole ever lets go of her hand - and if a time comes, she'll use it, but any real hope Katie had of leaving this building alive died with Alex. The thought elicits a kind of wary acceptance in her.

Fuck you, girlfriend. Suck it up and get your shit together. There's a world of kissing and breasts and heat out there, and with me out of the picture, you're just going to have to do them all for the both of us.

She sobs, once, the shock cutting through the growing numbness.

"Shhh. Shhh." The sweaty bald man is looking around nervously, waving his free hand in front of her face in a frantic calming gesture. She closes her eyes and takes a deep breath, focuses on not crying. She can feel it in her throat, painful, but she holds it in.

She feels a hand on her breast.

Her eyes fly open, mouth too, and the sweaty bald man lets go of her chest and clamps his free hand across her face. He does it hard enough that she's pushed back and to the side, her free hand falling flat against the ground behind her to hold her up. Trapped. He's above her now, eyes flicking between her face and her breasts.

"Sorry. I've never had anyone. I can't die like this. Sorry." He's whispering, face far too close to hers. A drop of sweat rolls down his nose and lands on her cheek.

"Just..." He yanks her held wrist, pulling her hand off of Alex, and pushes it into his stomach. With a low grunt of effort, he squeezes her hand down his trousers. She feels skin being scraped off of the back of her hand by the belt buckle and moans into his fingers. Her eyes flick from side to side, trying to see the rest of the congregation, but her neck is twisted to one side, and she can only see that the man and her are beneath the sight line of the bench.

She can see no-one.

No-one towards the back of the church can see her. Them.

"Just..." Her hand is flat against his lower stomach, trapped there by his bigger hand, now on top of hers, crushing. She feels short hairs brushing her fingertips. She gags into his hand.

"Just..."

She's stuck. He's moved over her, using his weight to hold her legs, and the angle she's fallen back to means she can't move her other arm without falling, banging her head.

Trapped.

Inside his pants, he interlocks his finger with hers, like a lovers grip. He rotates her wrist, and again she cries out into his muffled hand. Then her hand is clamped around something hot, hard and soft.

"That's it." His hand is clamped over hers, squeezing painfully. He starts to jerk, hard and fast. The skin on her lower arm scrapes against his belt buckle, scratching. His grip is tremendous, and she can already feel her fingertips becoming numb. His breathing becomes ragged, harsh. He sounds like he might be about to have a fit.

Please stop this.

She feels no anger, only a sick dread in her stomach, a yawning pit.

Please stop this.

His face is so close now that all she can see is his left eye staring into hers. She can see the tremble caused by the motion of his arm in his face. She can't seem to close her eyes.

His eyelid flutters, and the thing in her hand throbs, twitches, spasming, and he makes some kind of not-quite-groan deep in his throat, and she feels sticky heat on her wrist. He squeezes harder, and she feels the bones of her fingers groan in protest, and then his grip loosens.

She pulls her hand out quickly, trying to ignore the wet warmth that seems to coat it as she does so, and pushes him in the chest, hard. He sprawls back and off her, releasing her legs. She gets them under her, freeing her left hand, sitting up.

She has her back to the stage now, so she has a clear view of the boy with the gun and the door behind him. She sees other members of the congregation dragging the bodies from further down the aisle. She snaps her head around to the stage. The madman is there, looking down the aisle in her direction.

She looks back at the sweaty bald man.

He's trying to get up. He landed heavily, arms sprawled out into the aisle, and he's struggling to roll over and get his arms under him. As she watches, he does this, but when he puts his weight on his hand it slips against the smooth wooden floor and out from under him, and he flops back down with a grunt. Katie is moving without thought now. She reaches over for Alex, feeling for the pocket, the jar.

A weapon.

Her hands are shaking. The coat is big, and she loses precious seconds scrabbling under the jacket, looking for the secret pocket. She finds it at last, hand closing over the cold lid of the jar.

As she does so, a hand clamps across her wrist again.

She cries out in shock, head whipping around. The sweaty bald man is staring at her; teeth clenched, furious. She tries to pull the jar out, but his grip holds strong. His smile is twisted and horrible. She feels things start to go grey, like the world is fading out.

Then a blade appears at his throat. The grin disappears like someone flicked a switch.

"What seems to be going on here?"

Kings

atie can feel her heart hammering in her chest. She has a second to marvel at the feeling, the vitality of it. It feels strange. At odds with the numbness in her mind.

The madman stands above the sweaty bald man. Katie stares up at his face. He looks angry, and cold. So cold. He stares back at her, face an exaggerated frown, clearly expecting her to answer his question.

For an awful moment, she can't remember what he said. It's too much, overload, the circumstances and events piling up behind her eyes, threatening shutdown. She feels sluggish, dislocated.

Talk to the man, girlfriend. Give him the score.

"He... He made me."

She holds up her hand, seeing for the first time the pale fluid smeared across it. She hears the sweaty bald man draw breath but does not look down at him. Dares not.

She sees the madman's eyes change focus to her hand, widen in recognition, then return to her face. He looks at her for a long time. She feels her stomach roll over, wonders if she's going to throw up.

"Please accept my apologies. That should not have happened."

She notices that his shoulders are trembling, just a little. Her eyes follow the movement, and yes, the fist holding the blade is shaking slightly, vibrating the blade against the neck of the sweaty bald man. The man is crying, she notes with no feeling at all, fat tears rolling down his cheeks.

"You owe this young lady an apology, don't you?"

The sweaty bald man nods frantically, apparently unaware of how close the blade is to his throat. He eyes track left, straining to see the figure behind him. "I'm sorry; I'm sorry! But it's your fault!"

"What?"

Shut up, silly man. He's going to kill you if you don't shut up.

"You said we were all going to die, and I've never... never had no-one! And, and, I couldn't die like that, not having... And anyway, she, she's..."

He starts crying, huge sobs that shake his whole frame, and the madman has to move the blade to stop the man from cutting his own throat. It's an awful sound. Katie notices the front of his jeans stain dark as the man's bladder lets go. He's incapable of making words now, and instead he just wails, as pure an expression of despair as Katie has ever heard. She looks at her smeared hand (*soiled*, she thinks), and back at his contorted face. She feels bad for him. For herself. For all of them.

She looks back up at the madman. Realises with a nasty jolt that he's been looking at her the whole time. Waiting for her attention.

"It's not true, you know. Free will is free will. What you have been unfortunate enough to be caught up in is what happens when a man gives himself permission to indulge his worst instincts."

Look who's talking, thinks Katie, the irony of the lunatic's statement feeling like a physical blow. She hates him at this moment, far more than she feels anything at all for the stupid silly dead sweaty bald man. The madman turns his attention back to the man under his sword.

"I have no use for you, beast. You are unclean. I send you ahead. In dishonour."

"Don't."

The madman stares at her. She feels the sweaty bald man looking too, and the feel of his gaze makes her face itch unpleasantly. But she does not look back at him. She stays on the madman.

She watches him draw breath. Once. Twice. Then he speaks.

"Why not?"

"Because..." She tries to think, tries to remember why she spoke up, but it's all too much, the pressure and the fear and the grossness, and the dull pain behind her eyes, in her stomach, the bomb and the sword and the blood and...

"Katie?"

...and Alex. Her love. Here and gone. Forever.

"Katie? Why not?"

Her mind turns on Alex, and the girl in the chair, and the pregnant woman, and Mike, his lovely story and terrible end, and then she remembers, and she says, "Because I don't want him on my conscience."

Her eyes move back to her attacker. On his knees, eyes streaming with tears. Snot and drool running down his face. Urine pooling under his knees. Abject. Despairing. She makes eye contact, and waits until she's sure he's looking.

"I don't want your death on me. I don't want to see you bleed. I don't want to have to think about you for the rest of my life. I don't want to have to think about you ever again."

He starts to try and talk, stammers, spittle flying from his lips. She cuts him off.

"Shut the fuck up! Shut up! I'm not doing this for you. I'm doing it for me. Okay?"

Her eyes move back up to the madman, and she tries to make her voice soften. "Okay? I'm doing it for me."

The madman stares at her. His gaze is intense, face very still, brow furrowed. Katie stares back, trying to stay calm.

"Noble, Katie. I respect that. Truly, I do." He nods, and offers a small smile. "But it's not your call. I say he dies. And my will be done."

153

Katie feels her face fall, and the man wails, a long, high note, and the wailing is joined by other noises, pitching up and down, getting louder. The madman hesitates, and Katie has a moment where she feels a disorientation that threatens to become dislocation, feels the world drawing away, becoming distant, and just as she teeters on the brink, the flashing blue lights through the windows connect with the word *sirens* in her mind.

She closes her eyes and takes a huge shuddering breath. Sirens. Too many to be able to tell how many. Different types too, pitches clashing, so Katie thinks that means there's probably police and ambulance or maybe a fire truck out there too. She hears them get close. The sirens cut off. They are close enough, big enough, that she hears gravel crunching under tires.

She opens her eyes. The madman has gone. The sweaty bald man is curled in a ball on the floor. He is trembling, sobbing, head clenched tight between his own arms.

"Could the person who fired please identify themselves. I repeat, can the shooter please make themselves known. The building is surrounded. There is no way out. We just want to end things peacefully. Please acknowledge."

The voice is coming from inside the church, and Katie experiences another moment of disorientation bordering on panic, before she realises it's coming from the dead policeman's radio.

She stands up so she can see his body; *Andrew, his name was Andrew,* and she notices with no surprise that the madman is already crouched at the body, picking up the radio handset and looking at it.

"Hello?"

Nothing.

She sees him frown, then press the button on the side.

"Hello?"

"Officer Jackson?"

"No. Officer Jackson is indisposed."

"Who is this? Please identify yourself."

The madman looks up at the boy with the gun. Katie sees them communicate silently.

"Call me Isaac."

"Issac, is Officer Jackson there? Is he hurt?"

"He's here."

"May we speak with him, please?"

"No."

There's a pause.

"Is he injured? We know shots have been fired."

"He's fine."

"We'd like to speak to him to confirm that."

"No."

"Isaac..."

"I tell you what, let me save you some time. I'm armed. I have a room full of people here, maybe seventy people. I do not intend them any harm, but I am not going to let them go until nine o'clock. At that time, I will let them all go and give myself up."

Katie feels a surge of anger at that last that makes her feel nauseous.

That sad sack isn't worth blowing lunch over, sweetheart. Now, what have I got in my pocket?

Suddenly Katie realises that all eyes are on the madman and his friend. That they're both looking at the dead policeman and the radio, and the sweaty bald man is sobbing into the floor, and no-one is looking at her. She kneels down next to Alex, eyes moving quickly between her and the bald man, but he seems entirely out of it. She lifts back the jacket carefully, looking again at the pocket, wondering, looking back at the man. Then she reaches her hand inside, fingers touching cool metal at the top of the whatever-it-is, and from the madman, she hears

"Now, if anyone attempts to come in here before that time, I will start shooting and innocent people will die..."

And that's when Katie hears a guttural scream of agony from the floor in front of the stage, and every pair of eyes

155

in the church flips back in her direction.

Revelation (III)

eborah turns towards the scream. The woman is giving birth, Deborah observes, and it's just like on TV. She's covered in sweat and her face is distorted in pain and she's on her back with her legs spread and her husband is holding her hand, and it looks awful.

It's also means that all eyes are now looking in Deborah's general direction, and that could be bad, because she doesn't want anyone to notice that she's moved. That she is now positioned close to the aisle, at the edge of the stage.

"What was that? Isaac? Are there injured people in there? Isaac? Is someone shot?"

The tension in the voice comes through loud and clear, crappy radio speaker be damned. She looks back up the hall over her shoulder, careful not to turn her chair around, and sees that the young lunatic is not looking so good, suddenly. That smug expression that had recently crept back, the one he'd worn as he'd smacked her around the head in the bygone era of this morning, it's been slapped off *his* face, looks like. She can see him in profile, as he looks at the shooter, and she actually sees the panic jump from one to the other like an electric spark, and she feels a savage satisfaction.

"Isaac? Isaac, we heard screaming. Isaac..."

"Wait, just wait!"

"Isaac, if there are people hurt, we need to..."

"You need to shut the fuck up, or I *will* shoot someone!" The fear in his voice is unmistakable, and to Deborah, it's a cold drink on a very hot day.

"What do you think, Chris?"

"I don't know; I don't know. If they think people are hurt, maybe they'll rush us?" Voice trembling again. *What a fucking wimp.*

"Fuck, fuck, fuck! I just want... ah, fuck it, nine o'clock! Just five hours!"

"Hey, you said this was a part of it, remember? You felt it, so..."

"I know what I said. I also recall something about the distance between feeling and knowing, don't you?"

"But, you..."

"Just... Hello Officer? Yes, I'm afraid someone was trying to escape. I had to point the gun at them, and it made them scream. No-one is hurt."

He lets go of the button straight away. *Lesson learned too late*, thinks Deborah.

"Isaac, shots have been fired, if someone is hurt in there, you need to send them out right now. No-one has to die, just..."

"And no-one will if you just leave me alone. I just need some quiet time. At nine, if you don't interfere, I will..."

The scream starts up again, and he winces as he releases the button. *Quick enough?* Deborah strains to hear the voice over the lowing of the birthing cattle.

"Isaac? Isaac, it sounds like someone is hurt. Please let them go, Isaac. If you need to be left alone, just stay in there. Let the people go. We won't try and get you; you can stay as long as you need. But if you don't let the people go, we might have to..."

The yelling has died down again, and Deborah can see the knuckles of the killer turn white as he clenches the radio in his fist.

"You come *near* that door and I will shoot someone. You try and come in the building, I empty the fucking clip.

You sit tight, and this will all be over at nine. That's it; that's all you need to know."

"Isaac..."

"I'll check back in at seven. If you break radio silence before then, I'll shoot someone. Out."

The young man stands and spins, now facing down the aisle, looking towards the front of the stage. Deborah holds her nerve and just stares back. She has time to wonder if it would be smarter to drop her gaze.

His eyes hold hers, then slide past as he says, "Peter?"

The man squatting by the birthing woman half rises from his haunches, looks over at the killer. He is pale, Deborah observes, but he seems composed. She wonders how tight he's really wound. How close to snapping.

"Yes?"

"Is Emma... is she close?"

"Yes. Our baby is coming. It will be here soon." How he keeps his voice that even Deborah does not know, but there's raw fear bubbling under.

The young man glances back at his accomplice. Deborah sees them talk without words. He turns back. Points. For just a second, Deborah thinks he's pointing at her, and at that moment, she discovers she is nowhere near beyond surprise or fear.

This is an unwelcome realisation.

"Katie?"

Deborah sees the girl, huddled over the body of the woman who got shot, jump like someone caught her playing with herself. To Deborah, it is an unmistakable motion of guilt, but the young man is either too distracted to notice or too frantic to care, because all he says is, "I need you to go and help with the birth."

"I... but..."

"I know you're not a nurse. I know. But you care, and you tried to help, and I think Emma needs someone like that. So go and help her, would you?"

"I... Yes. Okay."

Deborah strains to hear the girl, read the tone of her voice — listening out for that note she'd heard before. Defiance, fury... something. Some spark.

Friend, foe, or more dead weight?

The young man turns back to his accomplice, and they start talking in low voices. All of Deborah's attention is focussed on Katie, and so she is the only person in the building to see Katie conceal something down the front of her trousers, pulling her T-shirt loose to cover it as she stands and turns around. The only one to see Katie wiping the back of her hand on the shirt as she does so, smearing something over the front of it, covering for the untucking.

Just in case.

Smart girl.

Deborah keeps the smile from her face through sheer will.

Katie fixes her eyes on the birthing woman as she heads over, so Deborah feels safe staring, but the shirt is too baggy, and she can't tell what's going on under there.

Frustrating.

Katie is in the aisle now, moving directly towards Deborah, head down. Deborah looks past her, sees the two psychos are still deep in no doubt riveting theological debate.

Katie closes, turns towards Emma, and Deborah, acting on pure impulse, kicks her.

Katie literally jumps, jerking her body away even as her head turns, and Deborah flicks her eyes back to the nutters, certain the movement will have caught one of them. But no, the circle jerk remains in place.

Lucky.

Eyes back to Katie, who stares at Deborah's leg then back at her face, mouth actually making a small 'o' of surprise. Deborah grits her teeth in frustration, taps her foot once, nods. *Yes, my fucking legs work.* She points at Katie's midriff, raises an eyebrow, cocks her head to one side. Katie blushes, and Deborah has time to think the girl has completely misread her. Then she lifts up her vest.

Deborah sees the top of a thin glass jar, lidded, tucked into the waistband of the girl's trousers. She can just make out the top level of a pink shiny fluid within before the white cloth drops again. She looks back up at Katie, nods. Katie nods back. *Good girl.* She turns and squats down, next to the woman, and talks to the man with her.

"How can I help?"

Deborah stares for a moment, and then her gut turns cold, as though something has gone horribly wrong, and it takes her less than a second in her heightened state to realise why.

The young man is no longer talking.

She looks up, feeling guilty as hell, and sure enough, the bomber is staring at her, eyes blazing, face twisted into an angry smile.

"What are you doing? Who said you could move?"

Luke

She feels the shape sliding into place inside her, deep in her belly, pushing forward now into her privates. The pain as each wave hits her body is the worst she's felt in her life, and each wave is closer than the last, stronger than the last, each new surge of pain is a new world's worst, and she feels as though she is being torn apart down there, stretched beyond breaking, and as the latest surge subsides she realises she is screaming and manages to stop, manages to peel open her screwed closed eyes, manages to find her husband's face, he is smiling and praying but he is scared, she feels it, and she sees it even more clearly in the face of the girl now with them, holding her other hand, telling her she's okay, she's going to be okay, a stupid mantra of ignorance from a child too innocent and too dumb to know what pain is, the way she herself had been before this, when she'd seen footage of women giving birth, thinking what a fuss they made and how dramatic they were being and how she was sure she'd be more stoic than that, more dignified, and now here she is on the cold floor of a community hall masquerading as a church, surrounded by strangers, howling like a wild dog passing her litter, and surrounded by fear and the smell of piss and blood, a madman with a bomb who will kill them all, her baby included, and still her body fights to shit this child into the world, a world it will have no time to even see or comprehend before it is pushed through to the next, and she wants it to stop happening, to just carry her baby inside, keep it warm within and free from sin until the end, and ascend together, but her own hateful biology, her traitor body, ah, that has other plans, that useless impulse to live, to survive, to have her baby, no matter the cost, no matter the point, and she reflects for a second on how stupid it is, how stupid we all are, dumb animals trapped by our natures into behaviours our minds know are futile, it's all fucking futile, she's going to die, her baby is going to die, scared and cold and screaming in a world that will never make sense, and she prays for God's mercy, and she prays for the end to be quick and painless for all of them, but especially for her child, and then her body heaves again, and there is only the pain, bright and savage and burning inside, as her body pushes and pushes and forces her child through her, tearing its way to the light and life and God-willing breath, and she is lost in the pain and the surge and screams just like the women she mocked in her mind, she screams in pain and fear as she pushes her child closer to birth, closer to death.

Ḣosea

Ḣatie's mind is spinning, slipping, as for the second time in the last five minutes her hand is crushed by the grip of another. *Emma, the madman said she was called Emma.* She tries to process what is happening, what may happen in the next few minutes. Emma is close, that much is clear, very close, and the girl in the chair is clearly planning something but now the madman is arguing with her, getting angry, and Katie is so scared. The argument had been drowned out by the screams, but as the current round of contractions passes, she hears it fade in again, like a weak radio signal.

"...theory of the scapegoat, Deborah?"

She swallows, throat dry and painful. *Not fair. So close!*

"Yes."

He smiles. It's awful.

"Because you seem like bad luck to me. So maybe..." The blade rises quickly, point a short thrust away from her stomach.

"Please, don't..." She feels the fear, making the blood pound in her throat. Making her voice wobble. She hates it.

"MAYBE..." The blade comes up, under her chin. She feels the skin in her neck pushed in by the point of the blade. "...I should just end it for you now."

"Please. Please. Don't." She's trying to calculate, to read him, but her instinct said to play it scared, so she did, and now she can't stop. Because she is scared. Because he's out of control now. He's lost, and angry.

He wants to kill her.

"Why not? It's what you want."

His smile shows teeth. It doesn't reach his eyes.

"Please put the sword down, please..."

It's all she can think to say – all she wants in the world, right now.

"I'm just giving you what you want. The release you crave so badly."

The blade presses harder. The pressure is still gentle, but feeling it increase is awful.

"I've changed my mind! Really, I've..."

Panic is close, now. She feels her eyes filling up.

"Deborah..."

"I don't want to die!" The tears start to spill down her face.

"Stop."

The blade moves quickly. The pressure under her chin is gone. Instead, a cold band lies across her windpipe. Her throat makes a small squeak, like a mouse.

"Don't you think it's strange that Mike couldn't stop me? That the priest couldn't? That this woman is birthing, that man went bestial just as the police turn up? Does it feel to you like an accident? Honestly, does it?"

He has no idea anymore how crazy he looks. How crazy he sounds.

"It feels... like a nightmare."

His grin becomes wider at that. Touching his eyes. She wants to flinch, to turn away. The cold steel at her throat negates the instinct, a mute denial.

"Right. Right! And in dreams, anything's possible! Don't you see? Did you ever marvel at a sunrise, Deborah? Ever look at dawn or sunset and feel stirred by the majesty of it?"

Deborah feels a bubble of anger rise at this. She grasps it frantically, a swimmer on the edge of exhaustion, reaching for driftwood.

"YES, okay? Yes, of course. Everyone does."

He nods, eyes focussed on some internal landscape.

"Right. Well, the sun is an explosion too. Just a ball of fire exploding and burning."

"So?"

"So it's just a matter of perspective. And anyway..."

"Excuse me?"

The voice is quiet and shaky, but it cuts through the babble behind Katie with its urgency, its *need*. She looks down at Emma, and sees her damp, scared eyes staring right back.

"What?"

"I think... I'm going to need you down there." Her eyes look down, then back up. "I need Peter to stay with me. Can you..."

"I'm not trained, I don't..."

"It's okay. You're here. Just do what you can. Will you?"

She is terrified. So is Katie. Her breathing is coming hard, like she's been running up stairs, and each inhale pushes the glass jar into her stomach. Alex's last gift to her. She feels strongly that she needs it, that it will be vital, somehow, but she doesn't know why or how, and she feels scared by it too, like its very existence in her possession is dangerous, marks her. *This is not a game.*

And this woman is so pale and so scared, and so brave.

"Yes, I'll do what I can. Do I... When the baby comes, do I need to pull, or..."

"No! No, just... cradle the head, gently. Tell us what you see. So I know."

"Yes, okay."

"Thank you. Peter?"

"Yes, darling."

"Stay with me, now, would you? I'm close now. Do you have the water still? For the... you know?"

"Yes."

Katie sees him hold up a plastic water bottle and shake it as she moves back, looking between Emma's spread legs. She's closer now to the madman and the girl in the chair, and their conversation begins to impose itself again.

"You could end all this, you could let us go..." The blade is still at her throat, but this last seems at least to take that faraway look from his eyes.

Deborah breathes.

"No, no. Deborah, we have to play it out, don't you see it? Don't you feel it?" Too much focus now, too much intensity as he stares into her face. She reacts with honesty borne of surprise.

"I just feel scared."

He nods, smile fading, but not entirely leaving.

"This too shall pass. At least you know the hour of your calling. It's a gift, if you really think about it. Something so few people ever get. There's a dignity to it, don't you agree?"

The sharpness of the blade is causing her throat to itch. It's infuriating, terrifying. He's going to kill her. Nothing can stop him. She needs a...

"Stop it! Please, just stop talking, stop this, this..."

Emma screams.

Katie has time to feel gratitude, even time to feel guilty for it, as the sound kills the argument. She feels their focus turn towards her and the scene in front of her. Katie watches with mute wonder as the lips of Emma's vagina peel back, and a dark coloured dome emerges. Emma's scream turns guttural, a growling yell that makes her whole body shudder, and Katie is aware that she's sat up, bearing down and forwards with her whole body, and the dome slides forward, slowly, and there's blood, and hair, Katie can see dark hair, stuck to the baby's head in wet clumps, and the scream dies down and the muscles stop trembling and Katie sees the dome disappear back inside, but Emma is wide open now, and surely next time...

"I can't do it! Peter! Please! Please, I can't do it, I can't, it's too much, make it stop, make it..."

"The baby is coming!"

Katie can't keep the excitement out of her voice, or the fear.

"I saw hair! It has hair! It's coming! Next time, I think..."

"Peter? Peter..."

"Baby is coming. Our beautiful child. You can do it..."

"I can't, I...

"...you can, you will. I love you. It's going to be okay..."

"No, it's... oh GOD!"

The word becomes a snarl, and it's all lower registry now, the growl of a wounded and desperate animal, and this time Katie sees it really is coming. That dome, streaked with blood, pushes out, and as Emma exhales with that fearsome sound, Katie sees the brow clear, and beneath it a wrinkled blue face coming into view. The features are horribly squashed together, and Katie gets a flash in her memory of pictures of old men gurning in competitions, but everything looks to be there, eyes screwed shut and a flattened boxer's nose and tiny lips.

"It's coming! The head is out, Emma!"

Deborah feels the blade fall away from her throat. She stares at the young man, his face in profile as he takes in the birth.

Emma comes to the end of the breath, takes in more, but the contraction has passed. Katie places her hands under the head, just taking the weight, no more. The baby feels hot to the touch, sticky. Emma sees it has blood on its face. There's more blood underneath, a steady stream trickling from Emma, starting to pool around Katie's knees.

"Next one, sweetheart. Next push does it."

Emma pants. Katie leans forward a little, kneeling in front of Emma, wondering why the baby isn't crying, worrying that the contraction has ended too soon and the baby hasn't arrived yet, terrified that she's made it go wrong somehow, the blue colour and wrinkled face looking damaged, and then Emma screams again, wordless, elemental, and Katie can see the pressure and strain in Emma's wobbling thighs, and more blood trills out from her, and just as Katie thinks that it's not going to be enough, that the baby is stuck somehow, the shoulders pop clear and the rest of the baby comes flying out towards her, a tangle of pink limbs streaked with red, and Katie has no time, is forced to react on instinct, and she keeps one hand under the head and the other moves under the body that's just appeared in her arms, like the messiest conjuring trick in the history of magic, and she holds the baby to her without thought, its body and head adding fresh red smears on the white fabric of her vest.

Katie holds the newborn baby in her arms, and for just a second, everything and everyone is silent and still.

The thin, hungry cry echoes throughout the silent church, and there's a ripple of reaction, murmurs, a couple of laughs. Emma is prone again, the last push having taken it all out of her. She's still in pain, and feels a terrible yawning emptiness down there, but the endorphins flood her system as she hears her baby cry, and the pain of her torn body barely registers. She holds her arms out from her prone position, and Katie hands her the baby, cord still sprung from the belly, and Emma lifts this, gently, then turns her head to her weeping, smiling husband.

Ezekiel

The killer places the sword on the edge of the stage.

He glances at Deborah, then slides it back, pushing it beyond her reach. His eyes turn back to the bundle of bloody pink flesh. To Deborah, he looks hypnotised.

Ezra

I t's a girl. We've got a daughter."

Peter nods, throat working, smiling fit to split, unable to talk. Emma holds the baby to her chest, feels the small form, so hot, resting against her, and she feels lightheaded. Dizzy, but elated. Her child. Her daughter. Here. Alive and crying. So beautiful.

She takes one of the tiny hands, lifts it to her lips, faintly surprised at how hard it is to do such a simple task, how heavy her arm feels, and she kisses the fingers.

"Sarah. Sarah."

She strokes the baby's head, then lifts her towards Peter. "Sarah, meet your daddy."

Peter takes the small pink/blue bundle carefully, and Emma feels her arms drop to her sides, exhausted.

Peter turns the child so Emma can see the length of her. He is weeping. She realises that her own cheeks are damp also.

Katie watches as Peter unscrews the water bottle with one hand, eyes locked on his baby daughter.

"I may not get all the words exactly right. I can't remember..."

"It's fine, Peter. It's fine. Let go and let God."

He nods, lips pressed together. To Katie it looks like he's suppressing a sob, and her heart goes out to him.

Then she feels movement next to her, and a figure squeezes between her and the edge of the stage. She turns and sees the madman. He is staring at Peter and the baby. Katie sees hunger and an awful eagerness in his face.

Peter either doesn't notice or doesn't care. He holds the baby carefully in his arm. The bottle ready.

"Sarah Annie Short, you are born in the sight and love of the Lord God, to loving parents Peter and Emma. Sarah, we ask that Jesus walk with you in your life, and that you know Him and love Him as He loves you."

The madman leans forward, and Katie realises his trigger hand is next to her, on the ground. He's using the fist for balance as he squats. Katie stares at that pushed in red button until it seems to fill her entire mind. She sees without registering the growing pool of dark blood that surrounds his knuckles.

"Lord God, we ask that you accept Sarah as one of your own, that you love her and keep her and protect her, first breath to last, bring her into your light, and that she serve your glory. We commend her soul to your loving care."

Katie feels the jar biting into her stomach as her breathing deepens, and still the madman is unaware of her attention, completely caught in the drama of the moment. She thinks. She hopes.

Because he's unarmed.

Suddenly, she sees this is her shot. Alex's shot. The moment. She can grab the hand, and hit him with the jar, and if she does it quick enough, and hard enough, and the girl in the wheelchair comes through, then maybe, just maybe...

"In front of this congregation here present, and in the eyes of the Lord..."

Katie places her left hand up under her shirt, gripping the top of the jar tight in her fist.

"...I baptise you, Sarah Annie Short..."

She rehearses it in her mind. Grab his hand first, then

pull and swing as quick as you can. One shot. Hope the surprise is enough, grip super hard. Pull out and up in one move. Hit his head as hard as you can. Maybe the glass breaks, maybe...

"...in the name of Our Lord God, and his risen son Jesus Christ."

...he falls, so fall with him, but do it, do it...

"May the Lord bless you and keep you, and..."

Now!

Katie's right hand clamps over the madman's fist, pushing his whole hand to the floor, and her left hand clenches as she rips the jar from her trousers. The adrenaline is singing and her muscles are over-tight from too much stress for far too long, and she's sucked her stomach in with fear, instinctively, so the jar is loose and fucking *flies* out of her waistband, and her arm is moving in the wrong direction, away from her body, and she can see the madman, scary-quick, turn towards her, face shifting through surprise and straight to anger, rage, and she brings her left arm forward with a frantic jerk, and the fresh blood and fluids and sweat that coat her palm cause the jar to slip back, so she's gripping the base, and as a stab of panic hits her she frantically tightens her grip, as hard as she can, and the momentum and the lubrication send the jar flying out of her hand, away from the madman and towards the aisle. She pictures it spinning in the air, over and over, away from her, and she hears it shatter, sees it in her mind, bursting over the mess where Alex bled out, sees the pink sparkles wash and mingle with the dark blood, and she doesn't really have time to feel misery and despair and heartache and loss and the terror of having killed everyone, but she feels it all anyway, as her gaze moves up to that pale face, those glaring eyes, the features twisting into a hateful smile, a grimace of triumph...

And that's when a sharp and bloody blade appears under his jaw line and pushes into his skin. Katie sees the smile drop, sees something that might be fear or only resignation flash in those eyes. She has time to think *finish it, sister. Send this man to Hell, and we can all go home.*

"I have very little reason to allow you to keep breathing. Resist my friend in any way, and I will open your throat. Clear?"

Katie sees the madman start to nod, feel the blade, wince.

"Clear. Now, look..."

"Shut the fuck up. One more word, *I gut you.*"

Katie clamps her empty hand over the full one, bringing all her strength and weight to bear, and as she twists around to do this, she looks up at the girl from the chair.

She's standing, long dark hair flowing to her waist. Her breathing is calm and steady. She's standing over the madman, the sword in her right hand at arm's length, and Katie sees it would take very little movement to act on her threat. Katie looks up to her face. She sees anger there, dark and terrible. They stare at each other. Nothing happens. The madman breathes next to her, and the girl does nothing. Katie feels something swelling up inside her.

"Kill him! KILL HIM!" The words are raw in her throat, painful. The girl only stares back at her.

And that's when she hears the sound of a gun being cocked.

"Put the fucking sword down."

Jude

Deborah looks up at Chris. Takes him in. She feels calm. Her mind open and aware like no time she can remember.

He's got the pistol pointed at her, gripped in both hands, legs braced. Like he's about to yell 'Freeze!' His hands are trembling. The gun is trembling too, the barrel wavering as it points at her.

She feels no fear. Only contempt, and this sense of heightened awareness, all senses on full.

"Stop, Chris."

His face is contorting, like he's trying not to cry. The tension of what he's done, what he's now being asked to do again, the emotional whiplash from homicidal to suicidal to calm, back to this – it's too much for him. He's so small, she thinks with no emotion at all. So tiny. So easily led.

"I... Put the sword down!"

"No."

He pushes the gun towards her in a jerk, but she is not surprised and does not flinch. He's not going to pull the trigger.

"I'll shoot you!"

"No, you won't."

"What? Yes, yes, I..."

"Do you want to know why you won't?"

Silence. They stare at each other.

"Look."

She points at her chair. He's too far away for her to rush him, but he takes his time just the same, cautious. She remains calm. Arm pointing, waiting.

Finally, his gaze flickers away, along the length of her arm. His eyes widen in recognition, and she sees a bunch of feelings cross his face, but only one matters to her, and it's fear. Maybe even terror. It's there and gone, behind the mask, but she knows it's what is in his mind.

"That's my wheelchair. I've sat in it, or a version of it, for seven years. Seven years, Chris."

His throat works, like he's trying to find something to say. She ploughs on, calm and even, but relentless.

"It was a spinal injury. Hit and run. Chris, I was never going to walk again."

She lets the moment hang. He's beyond speech now. She sees his eyes fill with water, a single drop escaping from his left eye. From beneath her, she hears an animal groan. She moves the blade a fraction of an inch and the groan cuts off with a squeak that on any other day would be hilarious.

"My spinal column was severed. That's irreversible. Irreparable. There was no fix. There is no fix."

The lies flow easily, mixing with the truth, indistinguishable. She gestures up and down the length of her body with her free left hand.

"And yet. Here I stand. Here I stand, Chris. In this house of the Lord, in the year nineteen ninety five, you are witness. The sick have been healed. The crippled walk."

Words she's heard a thousand times, prayed over, raged over, words that have caused bile to rise in her throat as another promise breaks, as all the promises break, endlessly, uselessly, like the useless faith beneath them, they flow out of her like water, clear and pure and easy. She sees Chris sobbing openly now, gun lowering, one hand swatting uselessly at his wet cheeks. She feels only a cold and distant contempt.

"What do you call that, Chris? What would you say this is?"

She waits. She can afford to. This is over. The young man on the end of her blade knew it from the first tear, and oh how he must be suffering now, twisting, and Deborah thinks that Katie might just need some help on that trigger now, because this is game over, and she's sure 'Isaac' is a terrible loser.

She waits and stares at Chris. He clears his throat once, twice. Looks down, away, up, then back, but he can't hold her gaze, looks down and away again.

"It's a miracle."

His voice is low, but clear. It carries. Deborah hears a ripple through the crowd.

Cattle.

"I'm sorry! I..."

She holds up her left hand, index finger up, and he quiets at once.

"All part of the plan."

"How..." He can't think how to formulate the sentence. She sees it, sees the strain on his mind, and she stays calm and quiet and neutral, knowing he'll figure it out.

Time ticks by. She's aware of everything around her. The baby making sucking noises, already on the teat, the ragged breathing of her captive, the girl holding the trigger, the still-shallow panting of the new mother, and beyond that circle the breaths and sighs and creaks of the multitude. She feels as though she can hear their thoughts, their minds crying out as one. *Help. Save us. Deliver us.* She manages not to smile. Free will.

It's a few minutes, it's a million years, it doesn't matter. She is calm and in control, and eventually he says, as she knows he must,

"What do you want me to do?"

There's another sigh at this, and a couple of maybe-coughs, maybe-yelps, maybe-sobs, and Deborah sends out the originators of those sounds murder thoughts, but her face remains neutral as she says

"Point the gun at Isaac. Shoot him if he so much as twitches."

Chris does so immediately. Deborah feels a surge of pleasure deep in her stomach, something slippery and sensual. Primal.

She kneels down behind her captive. The bomber, the lunatic. The loser. He is frozen with fear, the one sure thing he had taken from him for good, forever, and she knows what she's about to do is pointless, an act of purest malice, but she cannot stop herself.

She leans in close to his head, lips close enough to his ear that she is almost kissing him. He stinks of sweat, sour and acrid. It is the smell of the defeated, and she inhales deeply through her nose, savouring it.

"I don't care why you did this. Do you hear me? I. Don't. Care. There are no reasons. Only will. *My* will be done. What is left of you can be measured in minutes. Seconds. God is real, and He couldn't care less about any of this. This is the end. Feel it. Know it."

The words are not spoken but exhaled into his ear, travelling only to his mind, and she sees the hairs of the back of his neck stand to attention, his breathing elevate, and she feels that low surge again. She turns away to stand, and her eyes meet Emma, staring at her with fear and confusion. Deborah holds her gaze and closes the eye that Chris cannot see in a slow wink. She sees confusion cross Katie's face as Deborah stands, removes the blade from Isaac's throat, and steps into the aisle. Chris moves into her place, gun barrel pressed into the top of the kneeling bomber's head.

Deborah nods. She looks up, over the congregation, all eyes save the two killers now on her. She resists the urge to spread her arms and strike a pose. To laugh.

She looks back, one last time, at the woman and the baby and the father and the killer and the gunman and the dumb girl. Soaking in the tableau, fixing it in her mind.

The kneeling figures. The pool of dark blood. Spreading...

"Emma? Emma, honey?"

Exodus (I)

Deborah looks back at the mother. Sees the sheet white of her face, the slackness of her jaw. Her body is limp, not even cradling the baby at her breast as it guzzles, blissfully unaware.

The baby.

Her husband keeps saying her name, the same concerned, calm voice, like a broken record, the same gentle shake of her shoulder, over and over. *Not a man, at this moment,* thinks Deborah – some kind of broken robot, internal circuit out of true, looping uselessly.

The words ring out, marked by an oppressive, shattered silence. It seems to Deborah that the words fall into that silence, passing through it without leaving a mark.

Her eyes turn to the baby, to the cable that still runs from the child to the mother. Inside the mother.

The baby.

Her baby.

Her *miracle.*

She reaches a decision.

She steps past Chris, around the sweaty bomber and the desperate girl gripping his fist. She kneels next to the husband. He continues saying his dead wife's name, gently, shaking her as if to wake her from an afternoon nap.

"Peter." She rests her free hand on his shoulder as she speaks. Peter turns to her, slowly. His face shows concern, but nothing more.

"Peter, we need to cut the cord. It's not good for the baby."

"Sarah."

"Yes. It's not good for Sarah to stay on the cord. We need to cut it, or she might get sick. Do you understand?"

"Yes, I... I was going to do it, but..."

"It's okay, Peter. I can do it. I just need you to hold Sarah while I do it. Can you do that?"

Peter nods. He reaches for the feeding baby, hesitates, then says,

"Sorry kiddo. Let's just give your mum a rest, shall we?"

His voice quavers on the word rest, but otherwise he is calm as he takes the child back into his arms. Those high thin cries begin again. Hunger. Fear.

Deborah reaches past Peter, takes the cable in her hand. It is sticky and warm to the touch. She squeezes a loop together and places the blade inside it. She looks up at the bomber, but his gaze is fixed ahead and vacant, face frozen. The beads of sweat and shallow breaths give the only clue of life. Nevertheless, Deborah looks at him as she flexes her arm, slicing through the thick flesh with a grunt of effort.

A small jet of near black fluid squirts from the open cord, spilling over the mother's chest. Peter does not see this, bouncing the bundle in his arms, making shushing noises, smiling distractedly. Deborah thinks it's the most awful thing she's ever seen.

"Peter?"

He looks up at her. His eyes are still dry, face still politely concerned.

"Yes?"

"I think Sarah needs to leave here. Don't you?"

She sees a smile ghost onto his face, flicker and die.

"Yes, but... Emma..."

"Emma needs your help. I'll take Sarah out, okay? Then once Emma is feeling better, you can both come out.

Okay? We won't be far – there's an ambulance just outside."

Deborah reaches her arms out as she speaks, ready to receive the bundle of squalling flesh. She sees a flicker of something cross Peter's face, a flash of thunder inside a cloud, but his voice is still even and calm as he says,

"Yes, all right. All right."

He looks down at Sarah. Lifts her face to his.

"I love you little girl. Mummy and daddy will see you soon. Okay?"

He kisses the baby's head, once, then holds the bundle out to Deborah. She places the sword carefully on the floor next to the mother, then takes the baby gently, cradling the head, but she does not look down at the child. She looks at Peter instead, trying hard to commit his face to her memory, to hold him in her mind just as she sees him now. She does not smile, and neither does he, but she nods, once, and he returns the gesture.

She stands. The way out is blocked, the two kneeling figures of the bomber and Emma filling the path to the aisle, so Deborah sits on the edge of the stage, then swings her legs around, before getting them under her and rising. She wobbles a little but does not fall, and has time to marvel at this.

Then she walks to the centre of the stage. She considers speaking, but she can think of nothing to say. Instead, she steps off the stage, into the central walkway. She takes a step, and whispers into Chris' ear.

"Count to twenty. Then shoot him."

She sees him stiffen, and their eyes lock – hers calm, his terrified, trapped. "God's will?" His voice cracks.

Close enough. "Yes." She holds his eyes for a moment longer, and he nods again.

She leaves him, leaves them all behind, walks down the aisle towards the door. Her feet carry her through the pool of blood and pink glitter left where Alex fell. Her footprints shimmer and sparkle in the afternoon sunlight that burns through the high glass windows. She passes the sweaty bald man, still curled upon the floor, sobbing into himself.

A second darker, stickier pool, where the preacher fell (*can I hear an amen?*), then she reaches the door. Keeping the child in the crook of her right arm, she pulls the handle.

The door opens a crack, but the body of the preacher stops it moving any further. She pulls again, harder, and he starts to roll, but then slumps back, pushing the door fully closed again.

Behind her, she can hear muttering, confusion, the first sparks of anger.

How fast is he counting?

She looks down, into the sightless eyes of the preacher. Sees her own face reflected back at her. She looks scared. Mad.

She yanks on the door, as hard as she can. Feels something twinge in her back, a little spike of pain. The preacher's body rolls further, onto his side, teeters on the edge of the centre of gravity, then starts to fall back.

She can hear more murmurs behind her, the first shuffles of movement.

How fast?

She hooks her foot under the neck of the corpse and pulls. The twinge in her back becomes a stabbing, ripping pain, and she grits her teeth, but finally the corpse moves, and the door opens wide enough for her to pass.

She does not hesitate. She does not look back. She steps between the doors and out into the light of the world. The corpse of the preacher rolls back against the door, closing it behind her.

Exodus (II)

There's a huge bank of police cars, vans, an ambulance. A fire engine, lights blinking in the early evening sunlight. There's a clamour of activity as she walks out, people in dark uniforms running about. She decides to take the initiative.

"He's letting me go! I have a newborn baby!" She holds the naked screaming child up and away from her body. On cue, it wriggles, reacting to the outside air, and she draws it back to her protectively. She sees a moment of conferring, then the man and woman near the ambulance gesture to her, calling her over. She walks towards them, quickly, words tumbling from her now.

"He has a bomb! He's got it strapped to him! He says he's going to set it off and kill everyone if..."

A pop of gunfire from behind her, then a roar, a great and terrible demon of rage, hot air pushing at her back. She staggers, trying to compensate for her increased momentum. Her vision catches sudden movement, shapes falling all around her. A huge lump of wood plants in the ground in front of her, she jumps desperately, then something solid connects with the side of her head and there is a moment of blackness.

The hard ground under her back is agony, but she can still feel her legs, her toes. Her eyes open. There are blades of grass growing down from the ceiling. Beneath it, there are the ruins of a building. The door has been blown out from the inside and also lies on the ceiling, and the roof is splayed outwards and down like a pair of hands held open. There are shreds of cloth and limbs caught on parts of the ragged architecture. She feels movement in her arms, registers that the child clutched there is breathing, howling – she feels hot exhalation against the bare skin of her arm.

There is no sound, only a single high note whining in both ears. A great ball of fire and black smoke falls from the ruins and rolls lazily down into the clear blue sky, falling towards the afternoon sun.

It is horrible, she thinks.

It is beautiful.

End

Acknowledgements

It has famously been observed that it takes a village to raise a child. Given that authors often refer to their books as their children, it won't entirely surprise you to learn this book has a number of midwives associated with it. In deference to the narrative you've just read, I will abandon the 'difficult birth' analogy there, but I would be utterly remiss if I did not thanks the following people, without whom you would not be reading these words.

Firstly, my critical readers, whose guidance, criticism, and judicious praise was, as ever, carefully balanced to ensure I get fixed what I need to get fixed without imploding with self doubt. For this novel, that includes David Baume, Samaya Lune, Carole Baume, Melissa Saxby, Rob and Jane, Marta Salek, Bruce Blanchard, Scott Lefebvre, Kayleigh Marie Edwards, Matt Andrew, Paul M. Feeney and Duncan Ralston. Every one of them helped make this book better. If it still sucks, that's all on me. And if I forgot anyone, well, I did warn you I suck at remembering names. Also thanks to Bracken MacLeod for the smell of gun smoke.

Similarly, I must give huge thanks to Ingrid Hall, a talented and straight talking editor who told me exactly what I needed to hear, not what I wanted to hear. Any errors that you find in what has proceeded is entirely a by-product of my stubborn refusal to take her advice.

Huge thanks and love must also go to Big Jim – Jim Mcleod, benevolent overlord of gingernutsofhorror.com, who took me on as a regular columnist in 2013 and whose passion and love of the genre is a constant course of inspiration. I'd also like to thank all my fellow Gingernutters, past and present, who have all provided inspiration of one kind or another along the long path to publication. It really does feel like family, you guys.

Huge thanks to The Sinister Horror Company, for agreeing to take a flyer on a fresh name – I sincerely hope this book lives up to your hopes for it, and regardless, I will always be grateful for the opportunity and vote of confidence. Special thanks to Vincent Hunt for the outstanding cover art and J.R. Park & Duncan P. Bradshaw for the additional line edit and formatting work. Y'all ROCK. Also thanks to Chris Hall of DLS Reviews, whose superb interview brought the book to their attention in the first place. Cheers, feller.

Thanks to Mark West, Nev Murray, Duncan Ralston, Daniel Chant, Jasper Bark, John Boden and Anna Belfrage for the advance notices - a novel lives or dies by word of mouth, so thank you so much for taking an early look at my work, and I'm so glad you enjoyed it.

Finally, thanks must go to my infinitely patient and long suffering wife, who has sat through all the mood swings, crises of confidence, nagging doubts, complaints about bloody characters not doing what they are supposed to, without ever once saying 'shut the fuck up!' That woman, ladies and gentlemen is a saint. Any success I have, I owe it all to you, love. Your support means everything.

Author Bio

Kit Power lives in Milton Keynes, England, and insists he's fine with that. His short fiction has been widely submitted, and occasionally published, including in Splatterpunk magazine, The 'At Hells Gate' anthology series, and most recently by The Sinister Horror Company as part of 'The Black Room Manuscripts' anthology. His short story collection 'A Warning About Your Future Enslavement That You Will Dismiss As A Collection Of Short Ficton: Not A Novel: A Novel' will be released by Double Life Press in October 2015. Those of you who enjoy near-professional levels of prevarication are invited to check out his blog at:

http://www.kitpowerwriter.blogspot.co.uk/

He is also the lead singer and chief lyricist for legendary rock band The Disciples Of Gonzo, who have thus far managed to avoid world-conquering fame and fortune, though it's clearly only a matter of time. They lurk online at:

http://www.disciplesofgonzo.com/

Also by
The Sinister Horror Company

Daniel Marc Chant

Burning House
Maldicion
Mr Robespierre

Duncan P. Bradshaw

Class Three
Class Four: Those Who Survive

J.R. Park

Terror Byte
Punch
Upon Waking

The Black Room Manuscripts, Volume One

Website:
www.sinisterhorrorcompany.com

Facebook:
www.facebook.com/sinisterhorrorcompany

Twitter:
www.twitter.com/sinisterhc

www.sinisterhorrorcompany.com

KIT POWER

Lightning Source UK Ltd.
Milton Keynes UK
UKOW04f2323161015

260736UK00001B/1/P